Preface

Ever feel like you're trying to do everything right, but nothing seems to work out for you? You attend church, pray, study the word of God, and constantly try to encourage others, but for you, everything continues to fall apart. Well, you're not alone.

This story is about a great husband, Andrew, whose life seems to be perfect until, one day, everything begins to go downhill. He does everything he can to stop it, but nothing is working for him. As he gets to the lowest point in his life, he begs God to soften his blow. In the midst of getting to this point, he also realizes that it has brought him closer to God, strengthening the relationship that he already had, causing him to pray harder, and pushing him towards purpose.

This story was written to advise all to remain hopeful even when it seems that God isn't listening, when you feel as if you are alone, broken, or defeated. Know that God is always there; working it out for you. He is a promise keeper.

To all of the women that may read this book, I know there are two things that we try to avoid if possible. The first thing is bringing the wrong man into our life. The second thing is losing the man that is right for us. My advice is to wait patiently, and never take your eyes off of God. In due time, God will show you who is right for you. Just make sure that you're right when he comes. The truth will always reveal itself.

Chapter 1

Andrew met his wife 10 years ago in a grocery store. It wasn't a pleasant meeting. She was in a hurry, and he was in her way. She roamed the aisles, searching for ingredients. He walked slowly, no list in hand, contemplating on what he would eat. This was very rare for him, being that he is man. Usually, he could eat whatever.

Eventually, she ran into him, dropping some of her groceries onto the floor. For just a second, he stood there, admiring her beauty. But, there was a hint of urgency and frustration in her demeanor, and she frowned as if she could have kicked him for being in her way. So, he politely bent down to pick up the groceries. As he gathered her items, she continuously tapped her foot and checked her watch. When he handed everything to her, she rolled her eyes, and ran to the check out.

Andrew is not usually that polite, but it was his day off, he was in no hurry, and she was beautiful. Although these things kept him calm, her behavior turned him off completely. She gave no eye contact, she was rude, and she was frustrated with him after she ran into him.

Oddly enough, two days later, they were both in the store again. He had forgotten to buy some hot sauce. She was buying salad dressing. Both items were on the same aisle in the grocery store. Therefore, they couldn't prevent seeing each other unless one waited on the other to walk away. As he grabbed the Louisiana, he noticed that she was watching him. He looked up to give her some of his own eye contact. She smiled. Her teeth were perfect, but he could only think of their last run-in. Therefore, he turned to walk away. Quickly, she rushed to him, tapping him on the shoulder. He turned to her, ready to brush her off, and leave the store.

"Hey, I'm sorry for being such a butthole the other day. I was in a hurry, and had run into the ditch to prevent an accident after someone had cut me off."

He turned from her, but she continued to talk.

"I know you probably don't care about that. I was just letting you know why I was in such a bad mood."

She turned to walk away. He tapped her on the shoulder. With her head turned in the other direction, she began to laugh. She couldn't face him.

"I was having a great day two days ago, until some lady ran into me in the grocery store. I tried to be polite to her because I realized she was in a hurry. When she started tapping her foot, I wanted to break every toe. But, she was beautiful."

She turned to him, blushing. He stared into her eyes as anger began to build in his own.

He continued, "So, I couldn't......you know, break her toes....Have a great day."

Nonchalantly, he turned to walk away. Noticing his expression, and understanding that her attitude had caused him to lose interest, she realized that she had to respond. She reached out to him, touching his shoulder.

"Stop....Please, stop."

He turned to her. Her smile had left her.

"I called myself an idiot all day after I ran into you. I wanted to take back everything I did. You had done nothing wrong. So, I thought this was my chance to tell you that I was sorry."

"And you did. I appreciate it." He began to walk away, frowning as if recalling that particular day upset him.

"Okay." Understanding his ill mood, she turned and walked away. She let out a sigh loud enough for him to hear. She knew her chances of seeing him again were slim to none. He was handsome, had an amazing build, flawless, dark skin, and was very clean-cut. His patience with her on their initial run-in caused her to have much interest in him. She wanted to kick herself, knowing that running into such a man doesn't happen that often. She continued shopping, fussing at herself all the while. He let her go, but stayed close.

As she walked to the checkout, he headed in the same direction, wanting to converse with her. He noticed the bag of charcoal in the cart.

"Are you grilling?"

"Yes."

"What are you making?"

"Lemon-basil, grilled chicken with fontina cheese."

"It sounds delicious."

"It is.... Would you like some?"

"Are you inviting me over to your place?"

"No, I was thinking that maybe I could meet you somewhere, and give it to you."

"Seriously?"

"Yeah, I don't know you. So, I can't invite you over like that."

"True..... Can you give me the recipe? Maybe I can make it myself."

She contemplated, but realized that giving him the recipe wouldn't allow her to see him.

"Where do you work?"

"What?"

"Where do you work? I was thinking that maybe I could bring it to you for lunch, depending on how close you are to where I work."

"In the Financial Center on 4th and Church."

"Wow.....I work at the dealership down the street from you."

"Oh.... What do you do there?"

"I work in the sales and marketing department."

"You don't seem to be much of a salesperson."

"What does that mean?"

"The last time I saw you, you were running me over, and your demeanor was jacked. Just can't see you, having that personality, and making a lot of sales."

"Okay. I'll take your criticism."

"What's your number?"

"529-7714."

"Okay, I'll give you a call later on, about to go watch the game with some friends. I'm already running a little late, but I wanted to chat with you."

She smiled, chuckled a little, and said, "Okay. Go and hang out with your friends."

"Bye."

After checking out, Drew rushed to his friend's house. He had already missed most of the first quarter between the Heat and Celtics.

The game had hyped everyone in the house, cold beer had been passed around, and everyone was standing, hoping that their team would win. Some had made bets on the game. Therefore, everyone anxiously awaited the end of it.

Andrew was in a pretty good mood after his team had won. He decided to call the lady he had met in the grocery store as he was headed home. He didn't realize they hadn't exchanged names until he was calling her.

"Hello?"

"Hi, it's Andrew, the guy you met at the store."

"Wow! We didn't exchange names...huh?"

"I know. Think we were both kind of caught up in the conversation. So, we didn't even think about it."

"Well, my name is Salida."

"Salida, what are you doing right now?"

"Taking the chicken off of the grill. Can you hold for a second?"

"Yeah, I can hold."

As seconds passed, he sat, trying to put her name with her face.

"Okay, are you still there?"

"Yeah, I'm here....I can't believe you're grilling this late."

"I started late. I was a little busy earlier."

"Oh, okay."

An hour had gone by, and they were still talking, chatting away about their hobbies, goals, places they would like to visit, families, everything. He found out that she's a part-time bartender, and makes cakes for a local restaurant not far from where he lives. Drew has a thing for hard-working women. Learning this about Salida drew him in. They agreed to have lunch the next day.

The next morning, Drew put on his favorite suit and tie, determined to make a great impression on their lunch date. They decided to have lunch outside, at the park about a mile away from her job. He had checked the weather during half-time the previous day. He knew it was going to be nice, with a slight breeze.

He went to work, anxiously awaiting lunchtime. For this reason, his day seemed longer; and lunchtime felt as if it were never coming. At 11:47 Drew headed to lunch. He called as he was pulling into the dealership. Apparently, she had been awaiting his arrival. After the first ring, she answered.

"Hello! Are you here?"

"Yes."

"I'm on my way out."

Seconds later, she was headed towards his car. Her dress swayed back and forth with every step. He got out of the car to open the door for her.

"You look nice."

"Thank you!" She said while blushing. "You look nice too."

He smiled, while closing the door. He knew she had dressed for the occasion just as he did.

As soon as he pulled up to the park, and shut off the ignition, she grabbed him, kissing him intensely. He grabbed her in response, pulling her close to him. Her lips were soft. He couldn't stop kissing her. She put her hands on his chest, slowly pulling herself away from him, obviously trying to cool down. She laid her head on his chest.

"Sorry."

"It's okay. I loved it." He said as he rubbed his hands over her hair. Her hair was soft and curly. It also smelled as if she had just washed it. He put his nose in her hair, just to get another whiff of the scent.

"Your hair smells good."

"Thanks..... I'm sorry for being so aggressive. You're so attractive, and I love your lips. I just wanted to feel them."
Her head was still on his chest. He wanted to grab her, kiss her uncontrollably. But, he's a gentleman. He decided to let her lead.
Removing her head from his chest, she began to open her lunch bag. She handed him a plate.
"I started warming this, at 11:57. So, it should be warm enough."
"Thanks....did you cook all of this last night?"
"Yes, I didn't want to just feed you chicken. So, I made broccoli casserole, garlic bread, and lemon bars for dessert. Hope you like it."
He was impressed. The food was delicious.

Lunch wasn't long enough. He dropped her off at the dealership, and headed back to work. Drew hated that he didn't kiss her as she got out of his car, but he didn't want to be disrespectful. He knew he would call her as soon as he left work anyway, maybe to meet up for dinner or something, or just let her come to his place.
Work seemed longer. Every hour, Drew picked up his phone to call Salida, but he stopped himself. He knew she had her own work to do. He tried to focus, but couldn't. He thought about how she kissed him when they were at the park. Her lips were soft. It seemed as if she hadn't been kissed in a while. As he worked, his mind drifted, wondering how long it had been since she had been in a relationship. There was also something about her demeanor at the grocery store, a sadness, or longing for something. Drew continued working, trying to stay focused in order to leave on time.
After work, as he walked to his car, his phone began to ring.
"Hello."
"Hey, it's Salida."
"Hey! How was your day?"
"For some reason, it seemed longer. I wanted to call you, but I knew you were working."
He chuckled at the thought of the two of them having the same thought.
"I wish you would have called me. What are you about to do now?"
"I was going to head to the park. It's a really beautiful day, and I would like to get, at least, three miles in."
"Are you running or walking?"
"I'm running, but I enjoy doing both."
"Okay, maybe I can bring my clothes with me next time. Then, I can run with you. Is that okay?"
"Of course," She exclaimed, while grinning from ear to ear on the other end.

He asked, "What are you doing afterwards? I wanted to see if I could whip up one of my specialties for you."

"Really?"

"Yes."

"So, you're going to cook for me?"

"Yes, absolutely. Would you like to meet me, or would you like to come over?"

"I'll come over. I want to make sure you really cooked."

He laughed aloud. "Okay, I'm going to show you. Just give me a call when you're on your way. I'm going to text my address to you now."

"Okay."

"Okay, bye!"

After hanging up, Drew headed to the grocery store. He needed to grab a few items. He also wanted to purchase a bottle of Moscato, thinking a little wine would go well with the Italian dish.

He went into the store, grabbed some fresh herbs, Italian sausage, pasta, and a few other ingredients. As he walked to the checkout, an older man approached him. "How are you sir?"

"I'm fine. And you?"

"I'm well. I just wanted to ask you to be patient with Salida. I noticed you two talking the other day. She's had a pretty rough time, and hasn't taken an interest in anyone after losing her child in this parking lot. Just be patient with her."

Drew was shocked, "Are you serious?"

"I'm afraid so."

"What happened?"

"Some idiot came by here, shooting. She had sent her son to the car to get a quarter for the gumball machine. When she heard the gunshots, she started running to get her son. As he came within arm's reach of her, the gunman shot him....... He died instantly."

"Did they catch the gunman?"

"Yeah, but he was under the influence. He was taken to a rehabilitation center. Then, he went to jail for about five years."

Drew clenched his teeth together. Anger was building in him.

"Damn! That's sad..... Man, thanks for telling me. I won't say anything to her about it. Maybe, when she's comfortable, she'll let me know."

"Okay sir. Nice talking to you."

"Same to you, have a great day."

Drew checked out. As he was heading out of the store, he noticed a cross drawn into the pavement. He had walked over that cross a thousand times, and never read it. Today, he walked around it, but couldn't read it. His heart was too sore. He tried to imagine how she felt every time she walked into the store.

Drew started cooking as soon as he walked into the house. While cooking, he tried to clear his mind, but couldn't. He's not the greatest person. He has taken advantage of a few vulnerable women, but he knew he couldn't do this to Salida. To break what had already been broken would make him heartless.

As he was cooking, his phone began to ring.

"Hello."

"Hey, I got your text. Was just calling to let you know I'm on my way."

"I must've stayed at the grocery store longer than I thought. You've already gone running?"

"Yes, and taken a shower, too. If you'd like, I can wait."

"No, I'll be finished by the time you get here. Plus, the food will be fresh and hot. So, you can come now... How far do you live from me?"

"I live about eight to ten minutes from you."

"That's not far at all, but you can go ahead and leave. The food won't be ready, but we can chat while we're waiting."

"Okay. Well, I'll see you in a minute."

"Alright."

She hung up, and sure enough, ten minutes later, she was at the door.

"Hi!"

"How are you?"

"I'm okay."

Drew held out his hand, "Come on in. The food is almost ready."

Salida stepped into the house, "It smells really good."

"Yeah, I saw the recipe on a coupon one day. I added a few spices to it, and loved it. So, I wanted to share it with you."

He turned to her. She smiled. As he turned to walk towards the kitchen, she grabbed his hand, pulling him towards her.

She's weak, he thought. *How could you take advantage of her, knowing that she's been through so much?*

Instead of kissing her, he picked her up, hugging her, while spinning her around. She laughed.

"Why'd you do that?"

"Just glad to see you. Have a seat. I'm going to check on the food. You can turn on the television if you'd like. The remote is on the coffee table."

"Okay."

"Do you drink wine?"

"Sure."

"Okay, I'll pour you a glass...... Are you comfortable?"

"Yes, are you always this nice?"

"I don't know. I hope so."

He poured her wine, and checked the food again. Everything was ready. He prepared the plates, and sat them on the table.

"Are you ready?"

"Yes."

"Okay, let's eat."

He pushed her chair up as she sat down. She seemed a bit startled by it. After walking over to his chair, he bowed his head.

"Let's pray."

She bowed her head, smiling inside, as he prayed over their dinner. When he finished, he waited for her to take the first bite.

"How is it?"

"Mmmmmm, this is so good!"

"Glad you like it. I also purchased some dessert. I love cheesecake. So, I bought one for us. Kind of wanted you to know what I really like."

She blushed, but seemed unhappy.

"Is something wrong?"

"No...well, I'm not sure. I just met you. I was mean to you the first day I saw you, but you've been so nice to me. Why?"

"I'm attracted to you. I knew you were having a bad day when I first saw you. I wasn't. It was my day off. So, I wanted to enjoy it. I can't hold that against you."

"I'm attracted to you too. But, you're really, really attractive, and respectful....why aren't you married?"

"I haven't always dated women that were right for me. I knew they weren't right. So, I never took it any farther than the bedroom, honestly."

"Is that what you want from me?"

"No."

"What is it?"

"Honestly?"

"Yes."

"You're beautiful, but you're fragile in some ways. It makes you even more beautiful. So, I just want to take my time."

He watched as she held her head down, slowly chewing her food, pondering his choice of words.

After eating, they stepped into the living room to chat. She turned to him before sitting on the couch.

"Dinner was great!"

"I'm glad you liked it."

"The wine was perfect with your Italian sausage dish."

"Yeah, it was. I make that dish, at least, once a month. I'll eat it until it's gone."

He noticed that her eyes were somewhat glossy. After sitting on the couch, he motioned for her to sit down beside him.

"You don't drink often, do you?"

"No, but I'm not intoxicated. I am a little tired. I made a few cakes when I came in from work."

"Do you want to lie down?"

"No, I'm okay."

"Come here."

She lied on his chest. He rubbed his hands through her hair until she had fallen fast asleep.

Andrew was a gentleman, taught to be that way by his father. He was also very compassionate. He knew Salida was vulnerable, but he also understood that taking advantage of her wouldn't help him. Instead, it would hurt her.

He awakened her. "Hey, I know you're tired. If you don't want to drive home, you can have my bed."

Salida was exhausted beyond words. "I'm sorry for falling asleep on you. Your home is warm, the dinner was great, and rubbing your hands through my hair didn't help, since I was already tired."

"I can't apologize for that. You were comfortable, and I wanted you to be."

He noticed that she was struggling to get it together.

"Why don't you stay here? I'll sleep in the guest room, and you can have my bed. There's a bathroom in my room. I have a t-shirt you can wear also."

"Are you sure?"

"Yes."

"You're giving up your bed for me?"

"Yes."

"Okay. I'll stay."

Andrew walked to his room, and grabbed a t-shirt for Salida. He also grabbed some clothes for himself as he prepared to sleep in the guest room.

"It's all yours." He said while handing the shirt to her.

"Thanks. What are you about to do?"

"Clean up my kitchen. Maybe watch another show."

"Okay."

Salida walked into the room, undressed, and put on the t-shirt given to her by Andrew. His room was immaculate, and smelled of his cologne. She slid into his bed, and fell fast asleep.

Andrew cleaned the kitchen, and sat down to watch another movie. Eventually, he too, fell asleep.

The next morning, Salida awakened, checking the time to see if she was running late for work. It was only 3:30. She thought Andrew would eventually come into the room, and take advantage of her. Honestly, she wanted him there. She hadn't been that close to a man in two years, and was hoping that she would wake up, and he was there.

She grabbed her pants, turned on the light, and walked to the bathroom. After making sure she looked okay, she headed through the dimly-lit house, looking for Andrew.

Andrew awakened to the sound of Salida's steps. "Salida?"

"Yes."

"Are you okay?"

"Yes. I was just checking on you."

"I'm fine."

"You're on the couch."

"Yeah, I fell asleep here while watching the show, got a little tired after cleaning up the kitchen."

He looked up at her. She stood over him, biting her lip as if she were stopping herself from saying what she wanted to say.

"What's up?"

"Will you come, and lie with me?"

"Are you cold?"

"No. I just feel awkward sleeping in your bed, and you're on the couch."

Andrew sighed, "Salida, come here."

He sat up on the couch, patting a spot for Salida to sit. She sat down beside him.

"I think you're very attractive. I've enjoyed your company. And, I want us to spend more time together. I'd love to sleep with you, but my attraction for you also makes me respect you."

Embarrassed by her invitation, Salida held her head down. "I understand. I don't want to have sex. I just want you next to me. Can you just hold me?"

"Right now, I can't. If I could, I would. The best thing for us now would be for me to stay here."

"Okay."

She stood, and headed back to the room. Andrew stayed on the couch, fighting the temptation to enter the room as he saw her return to the room in his t-shirt and her tight jeans. He truly wanted to go to his room, comfort Salida, and give her whatever she desired. But, he was resolute and knew that he wouldn't respect her as much if she allowed him to sleep with her.

Salida was unable to sleep afterwards. She lay in bed, wondering what was wrong with her to cause him to reject her. Unable to understand, she changed into her clothes, and headed towards the door.

"Where are you going?"

"I 'm sorry. I couldn't sleep anymore."

"Is my bed uncomfortable?"

"No. It's me. Being in an unfamiliar place, trying to rest....I just wasn't able to go back to sleep."

"I wanted you to rest. I was going to cook breakfast in the morning before you headed home."

Salida smiled, shaking her head. She couldn't understand why Drew was so nice to her.

He continued, "If you want to leave, I can't stop you. I can only tell you that I would love for you to stay."

She could see the sincerity in his face. He didn't blink. He just sat, watching her expression as well.

"Okay, I'll stay....Your bed is larger than mine. I get lost in my turns. But, it's okay. I'll go back to sleep."

"Alright sweetie."

Salida headed back to the room, took off her pants, and wrapped herself in the cover. She couldn't help but wonder how many other women had been there, lying in the same bed she was now lying in. She removed that curiosity, and started to wonder how long a relationship between the two of them would last.

She needed someone like Drew, someone respectful, considerate, amazingly handsome, loves to cook, and works. What little she knew about him, made her even more curious as to why he wasn't married. Salida eventually thought herself back to sleep.

Drew awakened at 5:30 to cook breakfast before he got dressed for work. He walked towards his room to check on Salida. She was still asleep, and wrapped in his sheets as if his temperature was on 40 degrees. For a second, he stood in the doorway, staring at her as she slept. He wondered what he could ever do to possibly hurt her. She was so innocent, so fragile, and so feminine. As he watched her, the image of the cross in the parking lot popped in his head. He turned, and headed towards the kitchen, trying to shake the thought.

Drew began to cook, he wanted everything to be perfect, and timed it so that all of the food would finish around the same time. He had also purchased fresh fruit while he was in the store so that Salida would have choices.

When the food was finished, he prepared three plates for her, put them on a tray, and headed to his room.

"Wake up sleepy-head."

Salida awakened to the aroma of the hickory-smoked bacon. The smell of the bacon overwhelmed the aroma of all of the other food. She smiled as she sat up in bed to view everything on the tray. After noticing the plate of fruit on the tray, she reached for a piece of honeydew. Andrew watched as she bit into it. Salida savored the sweetness. After swallowing, she smiled and said "Good morning!"

"Good morning! Did you rest okay?"

"I did. Where's your food?"

"It's in the kitchen. Would you like to eat in the kitchen or here?"

"I'll eat in the kitchen with you. Let me put on my pants, and I'll be in there."

"Okay. I'll take your food, and sit it on the table."

"Thanks."

He headed towards the kitchen with the food. She jumped out of bed, and into her pants. Quickly, she checked her appearance, and headed towards the kitchen. As she entered the kitchen, she noticed that he had already prepared a plate for himself. He was already seated, and had bowed his head to pray. She sat, and bowed her head also. She listened as he thanked God for the food, for allowing them to wake up to see another day, and for everything. He also asked God to bless everyone with basic needs. The sincerity in his voice as he prayed made her wonder what he had been through to humble him so. After he ended the prayer, she reached for another piece of honeydew.

"I see that you like honeydew."

"I love it! This one is perfect."

"Glad you like it."

"All of my food looks really good. I want to eat it without looking like a pig."

"The only thing that could possibly bother me is you not eating your food."

With that being said, Salida consumed everything on all three plates. Andrew did the same.

"I have more honeydew if you'd like."

"I wish I could consume more, but I'm full. It's 6:20, and I have to go home to shower before work."

"Okay."

Salida grabbed her purse, and headed towards the door. Andrew walked behind her. She turned to him.

"Thank you so much for everything."

"No problem."

After hugging him, she headed to her car. Andrew watched as she pulled away. He closed the door, and headed for the shower. Although he didn't have to be at work until 9, he decided that since he was awake, he could shower. Then, lie down for another hour of sleep.

Salida spent her whole day wondering whether or not to call or text Andrew. She wanted to give him space, and allow him some time to call her. She paced around the office, busying herself with loans, and avoiding everyone that would ask any questions about her lunch date the previous day.

Noticing that Salida was pacing, her coworker Chelsea walked into the office.

"Want to give me some details on the guy you left with yesterday?"

"Not really."

"Why not?"

"Just don't want to talk about it."

"Why wouldn't you tell me? You know I love to hear stories on hook-ups."

"I know, but I'm busy right now. I have so much to do, and you do too. We've had an increase in sales over the last few days, and there are probably just as many loans on your desk as there are mine."

"That's true, but I still have time to hear your story."

"Not if I don't want to share it."

"You're so wrong! How can you just be all private about this?"

"I'm not. I just want work to be work, and my personal life to be my personal life."

"Okay...well...I'm leaving your office now."

"Okay, enjoy the rest of your day."

Chelsea headed back to her seat, upset that Salida wasn't sharing her story. Salida continued working. Eventually, she closed her door, keeping herself preoccupied with work.

At noon, her phone began to vibrate. Andrew was texting her. Her text read: Been thinking of you all day. She smiled, and began to text him back: Thinking about you too. Call me when you get a chance.
She reached for her papers, but the phone began to vibrate again: K. Will call you when I get off. She replied: K.

For weeks, Andrew and Salida began to see each other every day. They ate, ran, and shopped together. On the days she bartended at the restaurant, he would stop by to eat with her on her break.
He realized that neither of them cared much for shopping. She wasn't the let's-go-in-every-store kind of woman, and he only loved to purchase ties. A new tie always seemed to make Drew feel as if he had new attire.
He loved being with her. Every day with her felt like a new day. He also noticed that the more he talked to her about himself, the more she opened up about her life to him. He wasn't the typical guy, and was willing to admit that he was far from perfect. Because of this, she admired him. Drew was humbled by his own experiences as well as the experiences of others. He was also a people watcher, and found much joy in the happiness of families. He was 31, and had no kids of his own.
 Drew loved kids. Every year, he and other members of his church would take the children to theme parks, swimming, hiking, or boat riding. He enjoyed the presence of the children, and longed for kids of his own. However, he felt that there was no one there to fulfill that longing that he had. No woman had been in his life that he desired to have children with until he met Salida. Drew was ready.
Salida lived in a single parent home, had been married once, and never talked about kids. She admitted that she hadn't considered getting married again, and never expected for her first marriage to end. She thought they were inseparable.
Drew asked, "Do you still love him?"
"Sometimes I feel as if I do. Other times I don't know what I feel. Circumstances tore us apart, circumstances that were beyond our control."
Drew noticed tears in Salida's eyes as he asked her about her marriage.
"Do you think you could get married again?"
"I'm sure I could, but I have a few things that I really need to work on."
"Like what?"
"It's kind of personal. One day, when I'm ready to tell you, I'll let you know everything."
Drew asked, "What do you think of me so far?"

"I think you're an amazing man, you're fun to be around, you're handsome, I love kissing you, talking to you...... Honestly, there's not anything that I don't like about you. Time will tell. I don't mean to say that as if I'm looking for something, but sometimes people become totally different from the person you first meet."

"That's true."

Turning to Drew, she asked, "What about me? What do you think of me so far?"

"There's so much to enjoy about you. You're beautiful, you get excited about the smallest things, and I love the way you bite your lip when you're nervous or when you're thinking. It's cute."

"How'd you notice that?"

"Just observing you."

Salida smiled on the inside as she softly punched Drew in his side.

"Why'd you hit me?"

"Just innocently flirting."

"Really?"

"Yeah," said Salida while unconsciously biting her lip.

Drew grabbed her, pulled her towards him, and kissed her softly. Kissing Drew made Salida feel weak in the knees. At times, she felt as if she was floating, and he was the only weight that held her down.

One day, as Salida pulled into the parking lot of his company, she ran into an old classmate, Jasmine.

"Jasmine?"

Jasmine turned towards Salida. "Hey!"

"Hey! I didn't know you work here."

"Yeah, I'm here. I've been working here for four years now."

"Wow! How have you been? I haven't seen you in forever."

"All is well. I'm headed to lunch. Would you like to go with me?"

"I can't. I'm waiting on someone. Maybe we can get together some other time."

Reaching into her purse, Jasmine pulled out a card.

"Here's my business card. Give me a call."

"Okay. It was great seeing you!"

"Same to you!"

Just as Jasmine was walking away, Drew opened the door to get in the car.

"Hey babe!"

"Hey! How has your day been?"

"It's been okay. What about you?"
"It's been great, sales are still up. So, we've been busy."
"It's always good to have sales."
"Yes, you're right."
"What would you like to eat?"
"I kind of have taste for Italian. How about you?"
"Italian's cool. I know just the place to go."

After seeing Andrew enter Salida's car, Jasmine called Chloe, one of the ladies in the office. For more than four months the two of them have made an effort for him to notice them.
"Hey girlie! What's up?"
"Is that any way to answer the office phone?"
"I knew it was you."
"Anyway, guess who I just saw getting into the car with one of my old classmates?"
"Who?"
"Andrew."
"Really!"
"Yes!"
"Damn! I thought he was gay!"
"I know. He never looks in our direction."
"What is she doing that we aren't? Is she pretty?"
"She's okay. I haven't seen her for a while. We used to hang out, clubbing every weekend, had some drinks, you know."
"What happened?"
"She got pregnant while she was in college, changed her lifestyle, and disappeared."
"Did she speak when she saw you?"
"Yeah, she let the window down. We chat for a while. Then, I left. He was right behind me, getting in her car."
"Did he speak?"
"No, he just got in the car, and she pulled off."
"Wow. What's up with that?"
"I don't know. I gave her my card to give me a call."
"You know, I heard he and one of the chicks in AR used to hit it off. I heard she left him because he couldn't satisfy."
"For real?"

"Yes, I thought that was the reason why he never tried to talk to anyone else."

"You know, it sucks when men aren't working with anything."

"Girl, tell me about it."

"Well, I have to finish eating."

"Alright, get with me when you get back."

"Okay."

After hanging up with Chloe, Jasmine felt a little relieved. Men always had a thing for Salida. She was beautiful, curvy, and charismatic. The problem was that, Jasmine desired most of the men that seemed to desire Salida. This time, she felt as if she had an advantage. Chloe was a gossip, and she always knew what was going on in everyone's life. Therefore, Jasmine was sure that everything Chloe had said about Andrew was true. For just a second, she smiled, thinking *finally Salida has a loser*. Jasmine also felt that she finally had a reason to talk to Andrew. She was sure that Salida had told him that the two of them used to be close. She decided that she would wait until most of the employees had left, and approach him. She no longer wanted anyone to think that she had an interest in him.

Eventually, Jasmine realized her lunch was just about over. She grabbed her things, and headed back into the building.

Salida and Andrew pulled up moments after Jasmine headed back into the building. From her desk, Jasmine watched as Andrew sat down to clock in. She checked her inbox to see if he would email her, letting her know that Salida informed him of their past friendship. There was nothing.

Two hours had gone by, and she had become exhausted with fighting the urge to email him. She had checked her inbox several times to see if he would email her. He didn't. Instead, he sat quietly, working diligently to balance.

She began to email him: So, how'd you and my girl meet? ...Afraid that he'd send a smart reply, she deleted it. She checked again to see what he was doing. He never looked her way. She spent the rest of her day at work watching Andrew, and checking her email.

Salida contemplated on calling Jasmine for a week. They kept in touch after High School, but spoke less and less over the years. Jasmine loved to gossip, flirt, and make herself seem irresistible. Constantly, Jasmine was always in a messed up situation that she, somehow, never knew she was in until it was ending. She knew what was going on in everyone's relationship, and made a mental note of the status of every attractive man she had ever considered dating. Salida had always kept her distance with Jasmine. Although, Jasmine was fun to hang around, she was a back-stabber. She was also devious, jealous-hearted, and a liar. Jasmine was trouble, and would do anything to ruin relationships.

Eventually, she called after trying to convince herself not to believe anything Jasmine would say. Salida knew the conversation would be long. Therefore, she waited until there was nothing left for her to do in the house. Jasmine answered, "Hello?"

"Jas?"

"Oh, what's up?"

"Not much. I'm just calling. I haven't seen you in forever. So, I thought that we could get together one day."

"Okay, that's cool. Girl, how did you and Andrew hook up? When I saw you two together, I was tripping."

"It's a long story."

"I'm sure. Everyone at work thinks he's gay."

"Really?"

"Yeah, we don't ever see him with any women."

"Maybe he's just picky, or maybe the women that he's dated aren't able to make it to lunch with him."

"I don't know. It's just something everybody thought."

"Wow... Well, he seems far from it to me."

"I'm sure he does, especially since you're seeing him."

"Yeah, he's a really nice guy."

"Maybe, I heard he's dated a few of the girls at work on the low... Well, not really dated, just sleeping around with them. Heard he had no package..... Maybe that's why he went outside."

Salida rolled her eyes. She didn't want to entertain the conversation. Jasmine continued, "I also heard he used to be a whore. So, be careful. Don't want you getting your feelings hurt for a loser."

"Thanks for looking out..... So, how's everything going with you?"

"Everything is great. Been dating this guy named Michael for a while. He keeps me pretty busy. He owns his own company, and travels often. Sometimes, I fly out to go and see him."

"That sounds exciting. It's great to know that everything is working out for you."

"Yeah, I know. Do you ever talk to Jonathan?"

Salida cringed after hearing that name.

"No, he has gone his way, and I've gone mine."

"I can't believe you two don't even talk after having a child together! I know your son is not here, but you and Jonathan were a team. He was so sexy when we were in school."

Salida fell silent as Jasmine continued nagging about her divorce from Jonathan. Fortunately, her phone began to beep. Drew was calling.

"Hey Jas, I have another call coming in. I'll call you back later."

"Okay girl. Call me back."

"Alright."

Salida hung up with Jasmine, but never picked up for Drew. She sat on her sofa, thinking about everything that Jasmine said. Overwhelmed by the conversation, she fell asleep.

Drew had called Salida multiple times, but she never answered. He began to worry that something was wrong, and headed to her place. When he arrived, he knocked on the door.

Salida awakened after hearing the door. She turned her phone on vibrate so that Andrew would believe that she never heard the phone ringing.

"Hi," she exclaimed as she opened the door.

"Hey, I've been calling you, became a little worried after you didn't answer. So, I came over to see if you were okay."

"I was sleep. My phone is on vibrate. Sorry.... Are you coming in?"

Drew noticed that Salida's demeanor was a little off. She seemed annoyed that he was there. He stepped inside, and began to walk towards the living room. He asked, "Are you okay?"

"Sure. I was just a little tired. Trying to clean up, and do a few things around the house.....what's up with you?"

"I really just came over to check on you."

"Well, I'm okay."

"Have you eaten anything?"

"I have eaten a little. I planned to go running earlier, but I haven't gone. Guess I'm just not feeling like it."

"It's okay to not feel like doing anything. Do you want me to go and get something for you to eat?"

"No."

"Would you like to be alone?"

"Right now, I think so. I have a lot on my mind, and I want to just chill."

"Okay, I'll leave." Drew headed towards the door.

Salida angrily grabbed Drew's arm, "Drew, what made you try to talk to me?"

Confused, Drew said, "Well, first, I was attracted to you."

"What was it about me that attracted you?"

"Salida, what's going on? Why are you drilling me on being with you?"

"Because, I don't want you playing with my feelings!"

"Have I done anything to make you think I'm playing with your feelings?"

"No."

"Do you want to tell me why you're asking me this?"

"No."

"Well, I'm going to leave. I don't like the way you're acting. Just call me when things are better for you."

"So, running away is easy for you when you're being drilled?"

"I'm not running. I'm just giving you space. I don't know why you're acting like this!"

"Don't yell at me! You've been whoring around you're little job, and now you're going outside of it because you've been with so many people."

"What? Who told you that?"

"It doesn't matter."

"It does. Some idiot told you that I was screwing around with people at work, and you believed it without even talking to me about it! If I really am that type of man, why didn't I just sleep with you when you stayed over the first time? You've been there several times after that, and I still haven't slept with you! What makes you so different if I was whoring around?"

Out of anger, Drew headed towards the door.

"Drew....stop! Please."

Drew paused. He hated arguing, especially when he wasn't in the wrong or was being accused of something he didn't do. He couldn't believe that Salida was even asking him questions regarding anyone from his job. He turned to her. "Salida, we've been dating for four months now. We've never slept together, and I have never, ever even thought of being with anyone else. I love you. I don't say it. I don't have to. I just do whatever I can to show you that this is how I feel. I don't know who you've been talking to, nor do I care. I just know that this should not be an argument between the two of us. I have to go."

Drew left.

In the meantime, Jasmine was sitting at home, trying to see what she could conjure up. She decided to call an old friend, one that could make the relationship between Salida and Drew a little more interesting.

Days had gone by, and Salida hadn't heard from Drew. She was furious with herself for falling into Jasmine's trap. She tried to wait for him to calm down, and call her. But, he didn't. She dialed his number.

"Hello?"

"Drew?"

"Yeah."

"I'm sorry."

"It's okay, Babe."

"Can I see you?"

"Right now, they're working on my car. Would you like to grab a bite later?"

"Yes."

"Alright, I'll call you when I'm leaving."

"Okay."

Salida breathed a sigh of relief after hanging up. For just a second, she thought she had lost him.

Two hours later, Drew called Salida, stating that he would be there in an hour. Salida began to get ready. She took a shower, brushed her teeth, and combed her hair. After putting on her clothes, she decided to dab on a little make-up, just enough to make her not look plain. The timing was perfect. Drew rang the doorbell just minutes after Salida had finished prepping. Immediately, they headed to an upscale, chill spot.

Twenty minutes after sitting down to eat, a man approached the table.

"Salida?"

"Yes." Salida raised her head. Her body stiffened as if she had seen a ghost. She closed her eyes as if that would cause him to disappear.

"We need to talk."

"How'd you know I was here?"

He looked at Drew, and turned back to Salida. "Can we talk for a second, privately?"

"I can't. I'm on a date."

"Salida, you're embarrassing me. I really need you to get up."

"Not now. I will talk to you after I finish. Why are you even here?"

Drew noticed that this man was not taking no for an answer. He had no clue as to who this guy was that was standing in front of them. He looked at Salida as if to ask "who is this?"

The guy on the other end of the table grabbed Salida by the arm. Drew stood. "Hey, that's enough! She said later."

"Drew, it's okay. I'll handle this.....Please sit," said Salida.

21

"Sit your bony ass down before I break you in half!"

"Stop it!" yelled Salida.

Drew remained standing. He was ready to pounce this guy to the ground. Both guys were cut and stood at the same height. The guy was a little larger, but Drew was fearless. Neither of them took their eyes off of one another. Salida looked towards Drew.

"Drew, please sit. This is my ex-husband, Jonathan. I will explain this to you later. I'm really sorry that this is happening."

Drew sat back in his seat. Salida looked at Jonathan.

"Baby, it's time for you to come home. I messed up. Blamed you for what happened. I was wrong. I know it's been a long time, but..."

"Jonathan, this is not a good time for talking. You barged in on my date with Drew, and you're demanding for me to talk to you."

"What does it matter?"

"I didn't come here with you. I came with him."

"Who is he? He doesn't even know you. He has no history with you."

He turned to Drew. "What do you even know about her?"

Drew looked away, pretending to not hear Jonathan, but a little frustrated with Salida.

"What do you know about her," repeated Jonathan.

"Jonathan, stop it! Please...please leave."

"Come with me, Babe."

"No."

"Come with me...please?"

"No, Jonathan. I came here with Drew. With Drew I'm staying. I will contact you later. Tonight, you have done enough. Please leave."

Jonathan walked away. Salida sat with her head down.

Drew had already handed his credit card to the waitress, and had their dinners packed. He was ready to leave. He was embarrassed, furious, and frustrated. He wanted nothing more than to end the night, drop Salida off at her house, and head to his own. He had nothing to say to her.

Salida could sense Drew's anger as they were leaving the restaurant. She never expected to run into Jonathan, especially on the night that she was trying to apologize to Drew about the episode that she had created the last time she had seen him. She was almost certain that she wouldn't see him again. She turned to him. "Drew, I'm really sorry for what happened tonight."

"It's okay. You handled it the best way you could."

"I tried. He wouldn't let up. Jonathan is a man that is used to having his way."

Drew turned to face Salida. "How about we just remain friends? I see that you have a lot going on. Obviously, you and this guy still care about each other."

"Drew, please don't do this to me. The past few days without you have been so rough. Not having you around has been horrible. Please don't do this. "

"Salida, I'm not used to a lot of craziness. This guy came in on our date to talk to you. He, obviously, believes that is acceptable. Before I move forward with you, I want to know that nothing and no one can come between us."

"He hasn't. If I wanted to be with him, I would have walked away with him. I didn't. I stayed right there with you."

"Okay, but how many more times will this happen?"

Drew opened the door for Salida. She sat with her hands covering her face. She had been embarrassed, and was extremely frustrated with Jonathan's appearance, but something told her that he didn't do this on his own. Someone told Jonathan that they were there. Otherwise, he would have never shown up at that place.

Drew and Salida sat in silence on the way home. Drew wasn't sure what to say. He just wanted to end the night.

Salida sat, thinking about what Jonathan had said concerning Drew's knowledge of her. She had shared almost everything with Drew, everything except her son's death. Just the thought of her son's death caused a lump full of wailing in her throat. It rushed through, making her stomach churn, causing her to let out a light moaning sound. She closed her eyes, and swallowed hard. She wasn't ready to talk about it. Going home sounded even better.

As Drew pulled into the yard, he turned to Salida, pulled her towards him, and kissed her forehead. "Love you."

"Love you too, Drew."

He walked around to let Salida out of the car. As she stood, she grabbed his hand. "I'm really sorry for what happened tonight."

"It's okay. I don't want to think about it. Let me walk you to the door."

Salida felt uneasy as they headed to the door. Days ago, Drew left because she accused him of sleeping around. Now, she has to explain why Jonathan showed up while they were eating. She wasn't sure she would ever see him again. With her emotions running wild, Salida fumbled for her keys. Drew stood back, ready to head home.

"I'm sorry, just a little frustrated."

"Do you need some help?"

Finally getting a grip on the keys, she said, "No, I have them."

"Okay. Well, I'll see you later."

"Drew, can you come in for a little while?"

"I can't. I'm a little tired, and just want to go home."

"Please....just a little while?"

"Salida..."

"Please?"

Drew gave in. Salida closed the door behind them, and directed Drew towards the couch. Drew sat, but she remained standing.

"Drew, something happened in my life that I have not been able to talk about. Just the thought hurts. So, I have it bottled up inside. Jonathan was my husband at the time. I really want to tell you, but... it causes my heart to burn."

Salida began to walk away as tears poured down her face, but Drew grabbed her, pulling her towards him. She began to sob drastically as he stood, holding her, causing him to hold her ever closer. He pulled her to the couch as her knees began to give way. He knew her story would be a hard story to tell. He never pushed her to tell the story. He planted kisses and rubbed his hands through her hair as she cried. His shirt had become damp from her tears.

"Hey Babe, let me get you some tissue."

Salida covered her face, while Drew ran to the bathroom. She tried so hard to gain control of herself, but couldn't.

Drew handed her the tissue. He knew he couldn't leave her this way. He locked the front door, and returned to Salida. They sat in total silence as he continued rubbing his fingers through her hair. Salida cried herself to sleep. Eventually, Drew had fallen asleep also.

When he awakened, he noticed that they were still lying on the couch. He picked Salida up, carried her to her room, and softly laid her on the bed, pulling the sheets slightly over her. Then, he removed his shirt and pants, and lied on the other side of her. They slept.

That morning, Drew and Salida awakened to her alarm. Salida hit her button, turning the alarm off. Drew rolled over. "Good morning."

"Good morning. Did you rest okay?"

"I did. Did you?"

"I did. Thanks for staying with me."

"Thanks for allowing me to stay with you."

Salida sighed, "Now I have to get ready for work."

"I know."

"I would love to not have to go in, and spend the day with you instead."

Drew smiled. "Do you have an extra toothbrush?"

"Yes. There are some in the medicine cabinet."

Drew jumped out of bed to brush his teeth. Salida watched as he revealed his physique. Turned on by him, but afraid that he would reject her, she threw the cover over her head, encouraging herself not to get out of the bed, and follow him to the restroom.

Drew was extremely hungry after not being able to finish his meal last night. He called out to Salida from the bathroom.

"Yes?"

"Want to grab a bite before you head to work? I am so hungry right now."

"We can, but I have to brush my teeth, and get ready."

Drew's stomach growled like a mad-man. He knew it would take a while for Salida to get ready. "Do you have anything to eat here?"

"Of course I do. Would you like for me to whip up a little something?"

"If you want, or I can while you're getting ready."

Salida sat in bed, smiling, "Dang, you really are hungry, huh?"

"Yes, my stomach has started talking. It's mad at me!"

Salida chuckled. "You're too much."

She was so glad that he stayed with her. Waking up next to him was always pleasant, especially since his fragrance was always on her pillows when he left. It made her feel as if he were still there. She jumped out of bed, and headed to the bathroom to grab her toothbrush.

Drew headed to the kitchen. He checked the refrigerator, and noticed that Salida had a really nice selection of fruit already cut. He ate fruit while preparing breakfast.

Salida's stomach began to growl as a whiff of Drew's cooking entered the bathroom. "That man can really cook. I'm going to gain fifty pounds if he keeps this up."

Drew finished cooking as soon as Salida stepped out of the shower. She put on her robe, and headed towards the kitchen.

"I don't remember having all of this food in my refrigerator."

"It was there...believe me."

After eating, Drew washed the dishes, and headed home. Salida finished getting dressed for work.

Drew decided against working. He was a little exhausted from sleeping on the couch half of the night. He also wanted to use the rest of the day to think. His run-in with Salida's ex-husband was far from pleasant. It was also a little uncomfortable for Drew as this guy was slightly larger. Drew had quickly fallen for Salida, and didn't understand what he could ever do to cause her to become so insecure. Therefore, he decided that he would seal the deal. He figured that he would take her to meet his parents for Thanksgiving, and leave a nice, little present under the tree for Christmas. He rested for two hours before preparing to go ring shopping.

Thanksgiving couldn't have come any sooner. The weather was great, and the fall leaves enlightened the peaceful scenery as the two of them traveled to the country. Drew had called his parents two weeks before their arrival, stating that he was bringing someone that he would like for them to meet. Both parents were curious as Drew hadn't been home for Thanksgiving in a few years. He was always working or traveling with friends around this particular time of the year. They were so glad to hear that their son was coming to visit.

Salida's mother was very disappointed and worried to hear that her daughter wouldn't be home for Thanksgiving. Salida had spent less and less time with the family after Christopher's death. Her mother always reassured her that God didn't make mistakes, but that was never comforting to Salida. She had created a wall for everyone to see. Her happiness was beyond reach, and her focus on her family begin to decrease more and more as her siblings began to have children.

Salida smiled and let down her window, enjoying the view and the breeze. She turned to look at Drew. He had been watching her off and on, checking her expression to see how things were with her. He smiled after she had let down the window.

"Ever been to the country?"

"No, I've seen shows about it on television, but I've never been. It's about ten times more beautiful now than it was on TV."

"Really?"

"Yes, I've never experienced this before."

Drew smiled, and continued Driving as Salida soaked up the atmosphere.

An hour later, Drew pulled into his parent's driveway. He walked to the door, knocked, and headed back to the car to grab their bags. Both of his parents came to assist him with his luggage. Drew's parents seemed really happy to see the two of them. They noticed Salida, standing on the other side of the car, appearing uncomfortably fearful.

"Come on in," stated his mother.

Salida walked behind Drew. She was nervous and excited.

As she entered the house, she noticed all of the pictures of Drew and his siblings hanging on the wall. She smiled at the sight of his football photo. She also noticed one of his prom pictures, sitting on a table in the foyer. Salida thought about her own youth. It wasn't as structured, her mother was always working, and the struggle to not get pregnant while in High School was insane. She and two of her other friends were the only three out of a group of fifteen girls that made it out of High School before having a baby.

Salida continued looking at pictures on the wall, while smiling and reminiscing of her own past. She stopped as she began to think of Jonathan. She then realized that she was standing alone in the foyer. She didn't know her way through the house. Therefore, she called Drew on his cell phone.

"Hey."

"Where are you?"

"Sitting in the living room, talking to my parents."

"You left me in the foyer. I don't know my way through the house."

"Actually, I thought you were still behind me, until I sat down to talk to them."

"Please come and get me."

"This house isn't that large. Can you hear me walking?"

"Yes."

"I'm looking at you now."

Salida turned around. Drew was standing in the hallway, grinning at her. She walked towards him.

"Drew?"

"What?"

"Why'd you leave me here?"

"You were looking at those pictures."

"I know, but I thought you were still there."

"Do you know how long you've been standing there?"

"Not really."

Drew noticed that Salida was nervous. She was biting her bottom lip, and her eyes were glowing. She looked like a lost kid whose parent had left her standing in the middle of the store. He held out his hand. "Let's go."

"Where are we going?"

"We're going to the kitchen."

The closer they got to the kitchen, the more she could smell the food. She didn't realize how hungry she was until then. "Ooh, that smells so good!"

"I know, my three sisters are here, and my brother is on his way, but we can eat. He's always late."

"Is everyone else eating?"

"Not yet. They were waiting on you."

Salida's stomach turned at the thought. "Sorry."

"It's okay."

They entered the kitchen, and to Salida's dismay there were, at least, thirty people standing around the table. Everyone was smiling, waiting to get a glimpse of Drew's friend. Salida held Drew's hand even tighter. She had never seen that many people at a family gathering. She and Drew walked to an empty corner of the kitchen, grabbed the hand of the person beside them, and bowed their heads as Drew's father began to pray. His prayer wasn't long. He literally blessed the food for them to eat.

After being introduced to the family, Salida found is easier to talk to Drew's youngest sister, Gloria. She seemed to be a little more laid back than the other sisters. She was also funny, beautiful, and soft-spoken.

Gloria had two sons, Joshua and Vincent. They were rowdy at times, but very respectful.

Salida asked, "How old are your sons?"

Gloria replied, "Five and three."

"Has the five year old started school?"

"He's in kindergarten now.... He's so smart."

"Really?"

"Yes, he has actually begun to read books on a third grade level."

"Wow! That's great."

Salida sat, watching the older son. Minutes later, she rushed to the restroom to clear her mind, and encourage herself to let go of her past.

Drew knocked on the door. "Are you okay in there?"

"Yeah, I'll be out in a second. Just wanted to make sure my nose was clean."

"Okay. I'm going to go outside for a while. Are you okay with staying in the house, or are you coming out?"

Salida opened the door. "I'll go outside. It looks really nice out there."

"Okay, come on."

Drew grabbed Salida's hand, and escorted her outside.

"Did you enjoy your dinner?"

"I loved it! I wanted to eat everything, but I was afraid they would put me out."

Drew laughed, "They would have let you eat. But, they also would have talked about your appetite when you left."

"I know."

Everyone was outside, playing different games or pouncing around in the inflatable. The teenagers and some of the adults were at the end of the street playing basketball. There was a basketball court at the end of the street, and people that weren't at the dinner had come over for the game. A very large crowd had formed in that area. A lady, that had come to watch the game, was now walking towards Drew. Drew and Salida were still holding hands. She had already checked Salida out before she headed over. "Drew!" She said as she came closer to the couple.
"Tamara! Hey, how are you?" Drew swept the lady off of her feet, hugging her tightly.
She displayed a flawless smile. "I'm great! I haven't seen you in forever."
"I know. Been a little busy."
After Drew let her down, she turned in Salida's direction, and held out her hand, "How are you? I'm Tamara, Drew's old neighbor."
Salida welcomed the handshake, "My name is Salida. I'm well! How about you?"
"I'm fine."
Salida could sense that Tamara was a little more than just an old neighbor, maybe a crush at some point in time. She was beautiful. She had long, dark hair, her skin was flawlessly chocolate, and her curves were in all the right places.

Tamara turned to Drew, "You're not going to get in on this action?"
"Not right now. I'll probably do something a little later. Going to show Salida around the place now."
"What is there to see?"
"A lot for someone that doesn't live here. I'll probably show her the old clubhouse too."
"Is it still up?"
"I'm sure it is, unless someone has been back there to tear it down. I think my dad has been keeping it up."
"I hope she has some tennis shoes."
Drew smiled, "She can wear mine if she doesn't."
Tamara asked Salida, "Did you bring some tennis shoes?"
"I did. I wasn't sure what I was getting into. So, I just brought some."
"I'm glad you did, but I would have brought some over if you needed them."
"Awe, that's sweet!"

"It's not a problem." Tamara began to walk away. "I'm going to get back to this game. I'll chat with you all later."

"It's was great meeting you," said Salida.

"Same to you! Drew, let me know if you two want to hang out later."

Drew smiled, "I'll let you know."

Salida watched Drew's reaction as his old neighbor walked away. He felt her staring. "What is it?"

"Who is she really?"

"She is my old neighbor, really. She's also a really close friend of mine. She's amazingly beautiful, but she's harmless."

"She is beautiful. How can you be close to someone that attractive without messing with her?"

"We have a totally different relationship. Behind all of that beauty is someone with an amazing heart. She loves healthy relationships. She would do anything to put you at ease. She knows that men watch her, but she wouldn't dare help one cheat."

"Wow. That's cool."

"Yeah, you have to love her."

"Is she married?"

"No. She dated a guy for a long time. He broke her heart really bad. Now, I think that she believes he's going to come back around, and ask her to marry him. Honestly, he doesn't deserve her. She was so good to him. I wish nothing but the best for her."

"Have you tried talking to her?"

"She doesn't talk to anyone about it. We all just know. She's tried to date other guys, but it never has worked out."

"Did you try to date her?"

"At one point, I thought about it. She's very attractive. When I tried to even mention it, she blew me off like a strong wind over a lit candle."

Salida laughed, "Is that country talk?"

"However you want to take it. She just let me know not to go there with her."

"So, you didn't try again?"

"No, plus I was cool with the guy that hurt her. He's not with her, but he's ruined every one of her relationships that he thought might lead to something more."

"Why?"

"He loves her, but he's doing his thing right now. At some point, someone is going to get a hold to her heart, and he won't be able to come back."

"I hope so. She's so pretty, and she offered her shoes if I needed them."

"Awe, so now you cool with her?"

"Whatever!"

They both laughed, as they headed back to the house to change shoes.

After changing shoes, Salida and Drew headed into the woods. Salida was afraid, but didn't want to admit it. She asked, "You don't have a small gun or anything, just in case?"

"Just in case what?"

"Just in case something walks up on us, how are we going to protect ourselves? What kind of wildlife is out here?"

"I don't know. I played in these woods for years, and never had any issues with animals."

"Yeah, but that was a long time ago. You don't know what has inhabited this area."

"Are you scared?"

"No."

"You're acting like it."

"I'm not. I'm just being cautious."

"So, if something walks up, are you going to protect me?"

Salida stood with her hands on her hips, "You're the man. Aren't you supposed to be the one to do the protecting?"

Drew laughed, "I got you, Babe. Stop worrying."

After walking a great distance from the house, Drew stopped, and looked around.

"What's wrong?"

Drew didn't reply. He continued looking for the small, orange "X's" his father had recently painted in the grass. He never looked up because he didn't want her to see the clubhouse until they were actually there.

Again, she asked, "What is it?"

He took ten steps to the left, counting as if he had hidden something in a certain area. Then, he stopped again.

Salida asked, "What are you doing?"

"He took six more steps to the left, and grabbed a rope that had knots. The rope looked as if it had been there for years. Drew pulled on the rope to see if it was still strong.

"Where'd you get that rope?"

"A guy that used to fish at the pond down the street from the house gave it to me a long time ago."

"That thing looks old. I'm not getting on it."

"I'm joking. It's not that old. Plus, if it can hold me, it can hold you."

"I'm not trying it."

"Okay, well, you'll be down here, in the middle of the woods, by yourself. Or you can take the steps on the backside of the tree. Plus, there's another rope in the clubhouse."

He handed her a pair of gloves.

"What am I supposed to do with these?"

Drew pulled another pair of gloves out of his pocket, and began to pull himself up. As he reached the top, he grabbed the other rope that was sitting in the clubhouse, threw it over a thick branch above him, and lowered it. It was stronger and cleaner than the other one.

"Grab this rope, and I'll lift you up here."

She grabbed the rope, and wrapped her feet around one of the knots. He began to lift her. She was so afraid that he was going to drop her, but also excited about being in a clubhouse for the first time. Once she reached the top, she finished pulling herself in.

"You're a little heavy."

"I know. I'm trying to lose a few pounds."

"You're okay. I've never had to pull a grown woman up."

Salida walked around, "So, this is where you and your neighbor used to hang out?"

"Yeah."

"What did you two do up here?"

"It wasn't just the two of us. One of my cousins and Gloria used to hang out with us."

"Oh. But, what did you do?"

"We talked, ate Little Debbie cakes, and played games. We had a ladder out here, but it had gotten old. So, we tossed it, and used this extra rope. There are steps on the back of this tree. I just always preferred the rope."

Drew watched as Salida took steps around the club house.

"Be careful. I'm not sure how strong this wood is. My dad said that he had come out here some time last year for the kids, and rebuilt the floor to make it safe."

Salida threw her hands up, "Why'd you bring me out here? We're high up in a tree, and the floor can cave in any minute!"

Drew laughed, "I'm kidding, the floor is really strong. My dad builds homes. So, even if the branches fall, the clubhouse will remain standing. He was out here a couple of days ago getting the clubhouse ready for the grandkids. I haven't been out here in so long; I almost forgot how to get to it."

Salida began to bite her bottom lip. "So, some of your nieces and nephews come out here?"

"Yes."

"This is a really nice clubhouse. It's also pretty big on the inside. Who knew that someone could build something like this on a tree?"

"Well, there are actually four trees holding it together. My dad does a really good job with the maintenance on it."

"I'd say."

Drew smiled, "You're really digging this, huh?"

"Yes, we didn't have a clubhouse, or anything close to this."

"I'm sure you had other things."

"We had an Atari, a Nintendo, and a few board games."

"You didn't play outside?"

"Not much."

"Wow, you really have been sheltered."

Salida nudged Drew a little. "So, what are we going to do up here?"

Drew turned to her, "Well, I wanted us to be alone in my favorite place. I used to come up here to just think sometimes."

Drew turned his back to Salida. He dug into his pocket.

"What are you doing?"

As he turned to her, he held up the ring that he had purchased weeks ago. She gasped, holding her hands to her face. "Oh my...."

Drew kept it simple. "Salida, I don't think I can live without you. I know there are some things that we have to clear from the air, but I do need you by my side.... So, will you marry me?"

"I will!"

"Really?"

"Yes, I will!"

Drew stood and kissed Salida uncontrollably. She returned the favor.

"So, this is why you brought me here?"

"Yes, I thought it would be great to propose to you here. It's quiet. Plus, I wanted to share something from my past with you. I was going to wait until Christmas, but now is better."

"That's sweet."

"I take it that you are ready to leave now?"

"I am. We're in the woods. It kind of creeps me out."

"Okay, we can leave. Do you want me to lower you down?"

"No, getting down should be easy."

Salida grabbed the rope, and slid down. Drew slid down afterwards. Then, hand in hand, they headed back to the house.

As they approached the yard, Drew told Salida that he was going to hang around to get in the next game of basketball.

"Okay, I'd love to watch."

"If you want, I can grab a chair so that you won't have to stand during the game."

"It's okay. If I get bored or hot, I'll find Gloria and chat with her for a while."

"Alright."

"Plus, I'd love to watch you play a game of basketball!"

"Really?"

"Absolutely! I can't imagine you playing basketball."

"Why do you say that?"

"Because you're so clean and reserved."

"What makes you think that?"

"You, your home, the way you dress, and everything else about you."

"I do enjoy being clean, smelling good, and having my clothes and house in order, but I don't mind getting dirty."

"I've never seen you dirty."

"We run together, and I work out."

"I know, but, even when we do that, you have a towel to wipe your face."

"That's so I won't get sweat in my eyes.....I don't have a towel on me now. So, I'll show you dirty."

"Okay."

Salida's observation surprised Drew. He loves to be clean and crisp, but he has no problem with getting a little dirty.

He walked over to a few guys that were standing around the court to check the status of the game, and see if he could play in the game to follow.

Realizing that Drew was getting in the game, some old classmates asked if he would join their team for the next game. Drew agreed. He walked back to Salida.

"I have to go and get my big boy shoes now. Had some old classmates that asked me to play with them in the next game. Those boys play like we're still in high school."

"Really?"

"Yeah, they take it serious. I have to stretch a little too."

Salida laughed. She had never seen a basketball court in the middle of nowhere, nor had she seen so many people come out for a game that wasn't being played at the school. She and Drew walked back to the house to get his shoes for the game.

The first game was almost over when they made it back. The score was 28-24. The first ones to make it to 32 were the winners. Drew walked over to his teammates, while Salida stood on the sideline. She noticed Gloria motioning for her to come and sit for the game. When she sat down, Gloria noticed the ring on Salida's finger. She grabbed her hand.

"Drew proposed to you?"

"Yes, he proposed when we had gone to the clubhouse."

"Wow! He must really love you. He's never taken anyone other than Tamara to that clubhouse with us."

"Did he like her?"

"I don't think so..... They never dated or anything. They always acted like siblings."

"She's very beautiful."

"Yes, she is, but she had been hurt so bad by her ex that she hasn't really found love again."

"Are you close to her too?"

"Of course, she's close to our whole family. She's closer to Drew than anyone because they were in the same class, and she didn't have any brothers. So, he always protected her. When she comes back, she'll probably sit beside me or my sister, Chrissy."

"Do I need to move?"

"No, she'll just sit on the other side. There's no need for you to worry about her, she's really cool."

Gloria's reassurance put Salida at ease. Tamara seemed harmless, but her beauty was undeniable and she seemed to be perfect for Drew.

The next game had started. The age difference of the team was noticeable. Drew was on a team with older players, but they played like professionals. The younger guys didn't seem to have a chance. The younger women stood on the opposite side of the court cheering, trying to motivate them to play harder, but they were no match for the older players.

Tamara had come back, and was sitting on the opposite side of Gloria. All of the people sitting on their side jumped up after every score from the older team.

The excitement from their side was beginning to annoy the younger side. The score was 24 to 10, and the older team had the ball. Drew had scored six points in the game, and was headed to the goal again. He went up for the shot. Before his feet could return to the ground, his opponent elbowed him in his diaphragm, and tried to knock his feet from under him. Drew struggled to land on both feet. Everyone heard something pop as he hit the ground. Tamara and Chrissy both jumped out of their seat, and headed to the court. Salida followed. Tamara went to help Drew. Chrissy and the rest of Drew's team rushed Drew's opponent. Chrissy screamed and yelled hysterically. Afraid, Drew's opponent fled.

Drew lied on the ground, taking deep breaths. The pain was excruciating. Tamara and Salida sat on opposite sides of him, comforting him. Salida rubbed the sweat from his face with the towel he had handed her. Drew's oldest sister, Anna, had already headed to get her car.

Tamara watched as Salida rubbed her fingers over Drew's head and blotted his face with a towel. Realizing that Salida was taking care of Drew, she stood to return to Chrissy. Chrissy was standing in the middle of the court, ready to fight anyone.

Tamara walked over to her, "Hey, I think all of the younger players and their friends are leaving."

"They better leave. I was ready to put a hurtin' on somebody."

"I know. You're standing in the middle of the court as if you're going to fight anyone that steps onto it."

Minutes later, Drew's sister, Anna, pulled up with their brother and father. They helped Drew to his feet, put him in the back of his brother's SUV, and headed to the hospital. Everyone else began to clear the court, and head to their homes.

Salida, sitting in the backseat of the SUV, looked back to check on Drew. She could almost feel his frustration. His foot seemed three times its normal size.

He could feel her watching him. "It's broken," he said to her. "I haven't been home for Thanksgiving in a while, haven't been here for six hours yet, and I broke my foot."

"It's going to be okay, Babe," replied Salida.

"Yeah, but now, I have to go to work with crutches. That's horrible."

"Maybe you should stay home the first few days."

"I'll consider it, but you don't know my manager. He'll find a way to ignite a flame with this, making my job hard for me."

"Let's not even think about your job right now. Let's get you to the hospital, see what's wrong, and enjoy the rest of our trip."

"There's not much for us to do with my leg being broken."

"I know, but we'll figure something out."

Salida put Drew at ease. He was so glad he had brought her to his hometown, and proposed to her. Drew wanted nothing more than to make her happy.

After an X-ray was taken, Drew found that he really had broken his foot. The doctor gave him some antibiotics that almost put him to sleep immediately. He was also given a cast and crutches that he was informed he would have to use for a long time.

Tamara sat in the living room along with the rest of Drew's family, waiting for an update on Drew. When the phone rang, everyone jumped. Drew's mom answered. Drew's father was on the other end, calling to inform the family of Drew's status. After his mom informed everyone, they all began to set a place for Drew on the couch, and add extra pillows to his bed so that his foot could stay elevated. Tamara, knowing that Drew loved fruit, had purchased all of his favorite fruit and dip, and sat it in the refrigerator. She knew that would make him feel a little better. Not wanting to invade on his time with his fiancée, she left.

Drew's brother backed the SUV as close to the house as he possibly could to keep Drew from having to use all of his energy to get into the house. Drew scooted himself to the edge of the trunk, grabbed his crutches, and headed to the couch. As he entered the living room, he noticed the spot that was already prepared for him. Drew felt sticky from the sweat that had dried on his body, but the antibiotics had overwhelmed him. Less than five minutes after he had sat down, Drew had fallen asleep.

Salida was sitting beside him, chatting with Gloria. She was also exhausted from the long day, but didn't want to sleep alone. She decided that she would take a shower, and return to the couch to be close to Drew.

The next morning, the family awakened around 3 a.m. for Black Friday. The noise throughout the house awakened Drew and Salida.

"Good morning," said Drew.

"Good morning....what time is it?"

"I'm not sure, but it has to be early since it's still dark outside."

"So, why is everyone walking around in the house at this time?"

"....Black Friday."

"Oh, I totally forgot about that."

"Yep, and my family goes faithfully every year."

"Are you going?"

"I can't. I'm on crutches, and I need a shower really bad. How did you even sleep close to me?"

"I didn't want to sleep in the bed alone, and I wanted to make sure you were okay."

"I'm fine. I'm going to get up and shower whenever they leave."

Drew's mother heard him and Salida talking. "Drew, how are you feeling?"

"I'm okay. I'm going to take a shower whenever you all get ready to leave."

"Do you need anything while we are out? You can write down what you need, and we'll get it."

"I don't have anything I really want to get, but thanks for offering. Are you all about to leave?"

"Yes, you know we're waiting on Keith. Salida, did you want to go with us? If so, we'll wait while you get ready?"

"No ma'am. I've never enjoyed the crowd. Plus, I don't have anything to get either."

"Okay...we'll see you two when we get back."

Drew waited until everyone was out of the house. "I'm going to jump in the shower now."

"Okay. Do you need help with anything?"

"No, I think I have it."

"What did the doctor say about being on your foot?"

"He said to stay off of it as much as I can so that it can heal."

"Well, you're going to need my help sometimes."

"That's true."

"And I'll be there. Just let me know what you need."

"Okay Babe, thanks."

Salida knew he wouldn't ask her for anything. His independence drove her crazy.

Drew headed towards the bathroom on his crutches. He hated them, but he didn't complain. The pain from his foot bothered him more.

Salida paced around the house as Drew showered. She couldn't wait for Gloria to return so that she would have someone to talk to.

After she heard the water from the shower, she decided to grab her phone, and check her messages. Her mother had called to check on her. She started to return the call, but decided that it was too early. Chelsea had also called, wanting nothing more than an update on Salida's love life. Jonathan had called four times the previous day. Once, he even stated that he had been by her mother's house. It was very odd that he called being that they hadn't spoken since the incident at the restaurant. Before that, he never called her. Salida sat on the couch contemplating. *Someone had to have been talking about me for Jonathan to call.* Although it was hard for her to admit, Jonathan knew he could get under Salida's skin at any time. They had an undeniable history. After the incident, he had nothing to do with her. Now, he's calling more than he had called in the last three years. She turned her phone off, and waited for Drew to return from the shower. Receiving calls from Jonathan left her on the edge.

Drew had planned to stay until Sunday so that he could take Salida to his home church. Breaking his foot made him want to leave sooner. He sat on the bed in the room in which he used to sleep, applying lotion, and contemplating on whether or not the two of them would stay.

The pain returned while he applied his lotion. He grabbed his pills that lay on the dresser beside his bed. After putting on clothes, he returned to the couch.

Salida watched as he struggled to make it to the couch.

"Do you need me to help you?"

"I'm okay. I just hate crutches."

"I know. I do too."

"You've had to use crutches before?"

"Yes, when I was younger. I tore ligaments playing softball."

"Really... How'd you do that?"

"I was trying to slide into second, when the girl at second fell on my foot."

"Was she big or something?"

"Very...I didn't know if I was hurting because she was on it, or because it was sprung. When they finally got her off of me, I just lay there for a minute. I felt like a cartoon character that had been smashed by a ton truck."

Drew laughed at the thought of Salida lying on the ground after having someone fall on her.

"It's funny now, but when it happened, it wasn't."

As she watched Drew, she noticed that he seemed out of it. "Are you okay?"

"I took one of those pills before I came in here. It's kicking in pretty hard."

"Well, go to sleep. I'll jump in the shower."

"Okay."

"Are the towels in the bathroom?"

"Yes, there's a linen closet in the bathroom. You can grab whatever you need."

"Alright."

"I'm sorry, but you'll probably be bored until we get back into town."

"I'm okay. I brought a couple of books I've wanted to read for some time now. I can catch up on those while you are sleeping."

"That's good."

"Get some rest. I'll be back in a minute."

Drew lied back on the couch. Less than five minutes later, he had fallen asleep.

The rest of the trip wasn't as boring as Drew thought it would be. Many of his old friends had come home for Thanksgiving, and stopped by to see him after hearing about what had happened to him. Some came by to get a glimpse of his sisters and fiancée. Friends of his siblings also stopped by to play catch up. Therefore, the house was always crowded. His parents were enjoying the company themselves. His mom made her famous punch, desserts, and finger foods for the visitors after all of the leftovers from Thanksgiving were eaten.

For a while, the traffic in the house was extremely heavy. Some were even standing outside of the house chatting. His parents set up three fire pits in the yard to keep everyone warm. As the day drew on, and it began to get dark again, they added lights to the patio to bring everyone closer.

Salida hadn't ever seen that much company in one house. She could only imagine what her mom would have said if people had begun to crowd their house the way Drew's parents' home had been crowded. She watched as his parents were glowing from the company. They seemed to enjoy every minute. At times, she had become exhausted from the traffic, and began to take brief naps as Drew chatted away with old friends.

Drew was also enjoying the company. He sat on the couch, catching up with some of his old teammates and their wives. He felt great when Salida was around. He was the only one of his friends that wasn't married or had children. Her presence, at least, ensured them that he was on the way. He smiled every time she entered the room. Some of the wives would even hold their husbands tighter, acknowledging her beauty.

Salida checked her watch. It was 9:30, and the crowd seemed to have been growing. She stood to search the house for Gloria.

"Where are you going, Babe," asked Drew.

"To look for Gloria...I was just going to see what she is doing."

"I think she's outside with Tamara."

"Oh... Well, I'll stay here."

"You can go and chill with them. It's not a problem."

"I'm sure she wants to spend time with her friends."

"I'm sure she wouldn't mind spending time with you also. Her friends are pretty cool."

"Okay, I'll go and look for her."

Salida walked away. She checked the front yard first, but didn't see her. She walked around the back, and saw Chrissy.

"Hey!"

"Hey, what's up?"

"I was looking for Gloria. Have you seen her?"

"Yeah, she's on the patio, playing cards with Tamara."

"Okay, I won't bother her."

"It's okay. She'd love to have a reason to get up. She's been winning all day."

"Wow! She must be really good."

"Yeah, she is, but most of the people that have been playing against her have been drinking. So, I don't think they know what they're putting down."

They both chuckled.

"Well, I'm going to check on her."

"Did you get tired of sitting in the house or something?"

"I did. Plus, I wanted to get some fresh air, but it is cold out here."

"I know. I just stepped away from one of the fire pits a minute ago. I was getting hot. There's another pit on the patio. So, you should warm up quickly. Mom and dad have been adding a lot of wood to the pits. They've also been serving hot chocolate with alcohol. So, they're keeping everybody warm."

"Your parents are really cool. They have been keeping everyone entertained all day."

"Yes, they love the company. They sit money aside every year for things like this."

"Wow, that's pretty awesome!"

"Wait until Christmas... It's even worse, and everyone gets gifts."

"Everyone gets a gift?"

"My parents don't want anyone to feel left out."

"That's amazing!"

After finishing her conversation with Chrissy, Salida headed over to the patio. Realizing that the patio was packed, she turned to walk back into the house.

"Salida, how are you?"

Salida turned back around to see who was talking to her. Tamara waved seeing that Salida didn't recognize her voice.

"Oh... Hi Tamara! I'm fine. I was looking for Gloria, but I'm a little cold. So, I was going to run back in the house."

"You can come and sit over here if you want. The pit is keeping everyone warm. Gloria just ran to the restroom. Mr. and Mrs. D are also keeping everybody warm with their hot chocolate. They are over by the grill. You should taste it! It's really good."

"I think I will try it. It seems that everyone out here is drinking it."

"Yes. It's good, but don't drink too much of it. Whatever they put in it will hit you when you least expect it. Then, you'll start sweating."

Salida laughed. "Has that happened to you?"

"No, but I've seen it happen to others. I'm not a heavy drinker. I have had some, but I know my limits."

"I understand."

Salida walked over to the grill to get her hands on a cup of the hot chocolate Drew's parents were serving. His mom saw her coming, and had already begun to pour a cup for her.

"Here you go sweetie!"

"Thanks! I have heard a lot about this hot chocolate."

"Yeah, we've been serving this hot chocolate for some years now. Everybody loves it. We just make sure everyone is old enough to drink it."

Salida laughed. She took a sip before she walked away. The temperature on the hot chocolate was perfect. It wasn't too hot to drink, but it was warm enough to keep anyone outside to endure the cold. The alcohol was barely noticeable, and added the perfect amount of flavor. Salida continued sipping as she returned to a spot beside Tamara.

"You were right. This is wonderful!"

Tamara chuckled, "I know. It makes you want to go back, and get more."

"Exactly, and the alcohol is hardly noticeable."

Tamara smiled. "How's Drew?"

"He's okay. He's sitting in the living room, talking to some of his friends."

"Okay. I know he hates not being able to get around like he wants. That man is always on the move. To have something like this to slow him down has to be frustrating for him."

"Yeah, you're right."

Salida sat, drinking her chocolate. She wanted to continue talking to Tamara, but couldn't think of anything to say. Luckily, Tamara asked, "How did you feel when Drew asked you to marry him at the clubhouse?"

"I was excited. I had no idea as to where he was taking me. When he asked, I think I jumped all over him."

They both laughed.

Salida continued, "Drew is an amazing man. He's very patient, he's handsome, and he's fun to be around. Meeting his parents and siblings yesterday was really scary for me."

"Why?" asked Tamara.

"I didn't expect them to be so warm and loving. They treated me as if they had known me forever."

"Yes, his parents are really nice. I think they would do anything to help anyone. I have watched his parents all my life. I've never seen them angry with one another. Honestly, I don't remember ever seeing them angry at all. When you see one, you'll always see the other somewhere in the vicinity.

They're inseparable. They're a couple to admire. Watching them causes you to long for that same kind of relationship."

"Well, I hope that things are that way when Drew and I are married."

"I'm sure it will be. Drew is a really good guy that came from an extraordinary family. Their morals and values are very old school. So, they are very respectful people."

"Yes, his family is very impressive."

"So, where are your parents?"

"My mom lives in the city, and I don't know my father. He was never there. I have two sisters and two brothers. We're close, but not like this family. We're respectful, but the environment in which we grew up makes things different. Drew's family welcomes any and every one into their home. With my family, this would have never happened."

"I understand. I grew up in a single parent home also, but my mother is very welcoming. The town is small. So, we all work together to keep the environment safe. Drew's father was like a father to me. There were other men that assisted in shaping the community, but he has really helped all of us."

"Wow, he seems to be a pretty awesome man."

"You'll see as you get closer to the family."

Salida sipped her drink as Tamara stood.

"I'm going to check on Drew. Are you going to come?"

"No, I'm going to chat with Gloria for a little while. Then, I'll come back in the house," replied Salida.

Tamara headed towards the house. As she stepped around the corner, she noticed her ex heading in her direction. She turned to see if she could quickly maneuver her way into a crowd so that he wouldn't notice her.

"Tammy-baby, you know I'm here to see you!"

Tamara turned, and smiled, "Hello Shaun."

He walked to her, wrapping his arms around her. She returned the favor, but slightly. His cologne left her mesmerized, and his arms around her small waist left her breathless. She could never understand how he was still able to have this effect on her. She had tried to avoid him as much as possible, but he always finds her somewhere. Tamara was melting. Shaun began to whisper in her ear.

"You're still so beautiful."

As cold as it was outside, Tamara was uncomfortably warm. Shaun continued, while rubbing his fingers through her hair.

"Can I see you later on tonight?"

"No."

"Why not?"

"Because, I don't want to see you Shaun."

"You do. Babe, you know we have a connection. I can even feel your warmth as I'm holding you. I want to be inside of you, giving you all of me."

He kissed her forehead; then, her cheek. Tamara's knees were slowly giving, but she knew Shaun was playing her. He always did. He seemed to get some sort of high off of making her look like a fool. Still, she would always give into him.

"Shaun, please don't do this to me."

He continued, "I want you, Babe. Every time I see you, I want to grab you, and remind myself of what I've been missing. You know I can't stop."

Tamara pushed herself away from him. Shaken by him, she picked up her pace to get away. He reached for her, but missed. Her walking away angered him. He ran to catch up. He grabbed her before she could make it to the door.

"Are you seeing someone?"

"No, I'm not seeing anyone. I'm just tired of letting you get into my head; tired of you ruining things for me. I've been in this town for several years too long because of you. All that you do is ruin my relationship with whomever I'm with. Then, you disappear."

"I'm not trying to do that. I just get caught up in other things, but I always come back for you."

"Yeah, only when you think I'm with someone else. Just let me go."

"Do you mean that?"

The look on his face made her rethink everything. She knew that if she gave in, he would stick around long enough to make her think he was willing to make things better: only to walk away again.

"I mean it."

He smiled, "You think you have balls now?"

"I don't need balls to tell you no. I know that you're playing me. You've been playing with my head for way too long. I'm tired of it. Please leave."

Shaun stepped back, "Is it Drew? Are you sleeping with Drew now?"

Tamara reached for the door.

"I knew it. Drew's been shady towards me since we broke up. That's cause he's screwing you. You're a slut!"

"That's enough," stated Drew's father as he walked towards Shaun. "You're making false accusations against her because you can't get your shit together. Get away from my house, and take your friends with you. I will not allow this to go on here."

Shaun said nothing. He and his friends got into their cars and left. Tamara stood with her head down, embarrassed by the scene her ex had made. Drew's father opened the door for her to step into the house.

"Thank you, Mr. D."

"No problem. That guy has always had some stronghold over you. I've never been able to understand it."

"I know. At some point in time, he made me feel as if his world revolved around me. I'm not sure what happened, but it stopped. He knows that I have never messed around with Drew. He was just digging for something to make me feel bad."

"I understand, but always know that he can only do what you allow him to do. You're not getting any younger. If he really wanted to be there, he would have been a long time ago. You're adults now."

"You're right. Please don't tell anyone about this, especially Drew."

"I won't. I'm sure Shaun won't come around here again."

Tamara hugged Drew's father. "I'm going to leave now."

"You don't have to go. Celia made some dessert for everyone. We knew that we would have a pretty big crowd."

"I do need to go, but I wanted to check on Drew first."

"Okay. Be careful going home."

"Yes sir."

Drew was sitting on the bed in his old room, when Tamara walked in.

"Hey, are you doing okay?"

"Yeah." Drew patted a spot on his bed. "Come sit."

Tamara sat beside him. "What's up?"

"What do you think of Salida?"

"She's cool. She's very pretty. I just talked to her for a while before I came in. So far, she seems to be okay."

"Yeah, she is. You know, I asked her to marry me at the clubhouse. I was going to wait until Christmas, but I thought now would be better."

"I saw the ring when she was rubbing your head on the court today. Plus, Gloria told me while you two were at the hospital."

Tamara looked for Drew's expression. He never looked in her direction. "Is there someone else in her life? Are you trying to rule out the competition?"

Drew said nothing. He sat, lock jawed.

"How long have you two been dating?"

"Not long.... I feel like she's right for me, but I also feel as if she is holding on to something."

"Do you mean someone?"

Drew nodded.

"Why do you feel that way?"

"Well, she was married before."

Drew checked Tamara's reaction. Tamara didn't flinch.

"Can you close the door so that we can talk privately?"

"I don't think that's a good idea with your girl being here. I don't want her to think anything."

"It's cool. She knows that we're close."

Tamara closed the door, and stood in front of the bed.

"Sit down. What is wrong with you?"

"Just don't want anyone getting any ideas."

"You used to never second-guess sitting on my bed. What's going on with you?"

"You weren't engaged then either."

"Yeah, but you're like my little sister. We've been best friends forever."

"If you really felt that way, how come I'm just now finding out about Salida?"

"I knew you had gone through a lot with your relationship. I didn't want to throw mine on you."

"But, if you're happy with someone, I think I should have at least known about it. You stopped calling me some months ago. I knew something was going on."

"I didn't want your disapproval. We said we would never get into a relationship with someone that had been married before."

"Drew, things change. We're older, and it's unlikely that we will find someone that has never been married."

Drew slightly agreed, "That's sort of true."

"I would still want the best for you."

"Okay. I still want to tell you about the run-in I had with her ex."

"If it's going to make me change what I think of her, you probably shouldn't tell me."

"If I can't tell you, who am I supposed to talk to?"

"How about the woman you just asked to marry you? Tell her how it makes you feel."

"Now you're asking me to put myself out there."

"No, I'm saying that if there's something about her that bothers you, you should tell her. Before you marry her, she needs to know what makes you uneasy. If she loves you, she'll do whatever she can to keep that from happening."

"You're right." Drew pointed his finger in Tamara's direction. "That's what I hate about you. You have all of the answers to work out a relationship, but the man for you seems to not even know that you exist."

"It's okay. He'll find me. Until then, I'm work in progress."

"What do you need to work on? I don't see anything wrong with you."

"We all have something that we need to work on. First, we have to see it."

"That's true. Can you believe that I haven't slept with her?"

"Now, that's a little hard to believe. You used to be a screwing fool."

They both laughed.

"I know. I just want this to be right. I know that she's gone through a lot, and I don't want her to feel as if she has to give herself to me in order to keep me around. I just want to be there for her."

"That's really sweet... I'm proud of you." Tamara patted Drew's back facetiously, "Look at you, growing up. You're going to be a real man, just like your father."

"Yep, I will someday."

"Well, I have to get out of here. I need to run in the morning."

"I wish I could run with you. I really miss those days, running six or seven miles, chatting with you about our future, and updating each other on the progress we were making towards succeeding."

"I know. You're there, Drew. Me, I'm still in this town, working at the same place, not growing."

"Just because I work for a huge company, doesn't mean that I'm successful. I still have a few things that I need to work on also."

Tamara was tired and ready to leave. "Okay, keep me updated."

"Are you going to church in the morning?"

"Yes, I will be there."

"Good, I want to hear you sing."

"What?"

"You know I love to hear you sing."

"Now you're asking for too much. Don't request any songs."

"Let's sing a song together."

"Why?"

"Because this is the only time I ever get to really sing."

"You're on crutches, your girl is here, and you want to sing a song with me? Are you trying to be a show-off?"

"No, but she's never heard me sing."

"Singing with me is going to get both of us killed."

"I'll see you at church."

"Alright, I guess."

Tamara left.

Church started at 9:30 on Sunday. Everyone left the house at the same time. Drew and Salida rode with his parents. Drew noticed Tamara's car as they pulled into the church parking lot. He smiled to himself.
Church had yet to start. Everyone shook hands, and settled into their seats. Drew quietly asked his mother to request that he and Tamara sing a song before church was over.
"I would love to hear the two of you sing! That girl has an amazing voice!"
"I know, but she won't sing with me unless it's requested. She used to sing with me in the clubhouse all of the time. I know just the song I want to sing."
"Okay, I'll tell Mrs. Taylor."
"Okay."
Church had begun. The choir sang beautifully, and the sermon was delivered perfectly. After the sermon, those that wanted to join were called to the altar. The pastor also prayed for the sick. Mrs. Taylor, then, stood for the announcements. Just as she was finishing the announcements, she stated, "I have a special request for Drew and Tamara to sing."
The whole church began to clap as the two of them stood. Salida was shocked to hear the request. Drew grabbed his crutches, headed over to the piano, and began to play. Tamara stood beside the piano, waiting to begin. As she began to sing, the audience began to stand. Drew joined in just in time. They sounded great together. Salida sat with tears rolling down her face as Drew and Tamara sang. Their voices were so sweet, so smooth. She had never heard him sing before, and had no clue that he could. By the second verse, the whole congregation was on their feet, even the Pastor was standing. When the song ended, Tamara walked back to her seat. Drew continued playing softly as the pastor dismissed church.
Salida walked over to Tamara after church, tears still in her eyes. They embraced.
"Your voice is beautiful."
"Thank you!"
"I didn't even know that Drew could sing or play the piano! When he stood to go up there, I had no idea!"
Tamara nodded in agreement, "Yeah, he can blow."
"He really can."
Drew headed over with the pastor as Salida chatted with Tamara.
"Pastor Moore, this is my fiancée, Salida."
"How are you?" asked the pastor.

"I'm well," replied Salida. "I'm getting to know more and more about Drew daily."

"Yes, that happens." The pastor looked around noticing others waiting to speak with him. "Well, it was great to meet you. You are always welcome to come and have service with us at any time."

"Thank you. It was a pleasure."

"I also want you to know that you're engaged to a man that came from a very respectful family. Mr. and Mrs. Davison have done a great job with raising their children. They've all grown up, and are doing well."

"I agree. I have never met a family so close. I have felt right at home since I've been here."

"Well, once again, it was great to meet you. I'll talk to you all later." Pastor Moore waved as he stepped away. "Enjoy your trip back."

"Thank you."

Salida stood back as Drew and Tamara said their good-byes. She was becoming more and more comfortable with the closeness between the two of them as she realized how close Tamara was to the whole family.

Mrs. D ran over to hug Tamara. "Girl, you sure know how to sing."

"Thanks Mrs. D!"

"I don't think anyone can stay in their seat when you and Drew get up there."

Tamara blushed. She was even more beautiful when she showed her bashful side.

Drew interrupted. "Well, we have to go now. We have to drive back tonight."

Tamara replied, "Okay, I'll see you all later." She turned to walk away. "Drew, don't forget to invite me to the wedding!"

"You know you have to sing in my wedding. Quit playing!"

Tamara shook her head, "Salida, it was great to meet you. Take care of my friend."

"I will," replied Salida.

Tamara continued walking. Drew and Salida headed towards the car.

After making it back from church, Drew and Salida decided to leave. Drew said his good-byes to the family as they assisted him with loading his things into the car. Twenty minutes later, he and Salida were headed back to the city.

Annoyed with his broken foot, Drew said, "I'm going to hate this six hour drive. It's going to be very uncomfortable."

"I know. If you want me to drive, I can."

"I might need you to drive later. So, you may want to get some rest now."

"I will…. Drew, how come you never told me that you could sing or play the piano?"

"I just don't think about it… It's not something I hide."

"Today was the first time I've ever heard you."

"I know… I don't sing on the choir at the church I attend. They also have a piano player. So, I just play at the house when I'm stressed. I sing in the shower."

Salida laughed, "Who doesn't sing in the shower?"

"I've never heard you sing. Can you sing?"

"No, I can't."

"Why don't you let me be the judge?"

"Do you want us to make it back safely?"

"Yes."

"Then, you don't need to hear me sing."

Drew laughed.

Drew dreaded returning to work that Monday. He called in so that he could get some rest. He also knew that his pain medication wasn't going to allow him to sit at work without falling asleep. After leaving a message, he swallowed a pain pill, and returned to his bed. He contacted Salida to let her know that he wasn't going in.

Salida answered after the first ring, "Hello?"

"Hey Babe, I'm not going in today. I feel really drowsy."

"I don't think I am either. I'm really exhausted."

"Do you want to grab a bite later, or you can come over?"

"I…I'm not…" As Salida was finishing her sentence, Drew heard someone in her background. "Hey Baby, where is …."

The line was dead. Drew called Salida again. The phone rang twice.

"Hello?"

"Is someone there?"

"No, my earring hit the button to hang up."

Drew sat quietly, waiting to hear the male voice again, "I can almost swear that I heard a man in the background before you hung up."

"My television was on. I just turned it off…. Can I call you back in a minute or so? I need to put some cakes in my car."

"Okay."

Salida hung up the phone. Drew sat on his couch, bewildered by Salida's lie.

Salida punched Jonathan in his shoulder. "What are you trying to do, ruin my life?"

Jonathan laughed, "Chill, Babe. I didn't know you were on the phone." He wrapped his arms around her. "Besides, what does it matter anyway?"

"It matters a lot. I just agreed to marry him!"

"Yeah, you shouldn't have done that. You know the two of us belong together." Jonathan turned Salida around to face him. "I was angry with you after what had happened to our son. You know how much I loved him. But, seeing you with someone else doesn't make things better."

Salida sat with her head down, "Drew is a really good guy. He came from a wonderful family. He's gentle, caring, amazingly humble..." Salida thought for a moment. "I can't think of anything bad about him."

"He's a punk! He hasn't even banged you, and you two have been dating for months. Now, you're calling me because he's not doing his part."

"He's not a punk. He's sympathetic."

Jonathan shook his head. "What are you going to do if he's sitting at your house right now? What if he knows you're not there? Huh?"

"That's not funny, Jonathan!"

"I'm not trying to be. I went to your mom's house, looking for you; and you were somewhere else, pretending to be Miss Perfect for Doug."

"It's Drew."

"Whatever."

Salida showered, put on her clothes, and headed to work. She called Drew on the way.

"Hello?"

"Hey, I'm headed to work now."

Drew looked at his phone in amazement. "I thought you weren't going in?"

"I know.... I wasn't at first, but I have a little catching up to do."

"So, did you drop the cakes off?"

"What?"

"The cakes?"

"Oh yeah, I...um... I dropped them off earlier."

"Okay. Well, I'm going to lie back down. My medicine is starting to kick in."

"Okay, I'll call and check on you when I am on lunch."

After hanging up with Salida, Drew called Tamara.

"Hey, Drew!"

"Hey, what's up?"

"Nothing, just headed to work."

"Tam, I know I've been taking medicine, but I'm not crazy."

"Why'd you say that?"

"I called Salida. We were talking. I heard a man in the background. Then, the phone cut off."

"Are you sure?"

"I'm positive. So, I called her back."

"Did you ask her about it?"

"She said that her television was on, but she also said that she was about to drop cakes off at the restaurant. The problem is that the restaurant doesn't open until eleven. No one is there. Then, she called me back to state that she was heading to work, but she had previously said that she wasn't going. When I asked her about dropping off the cakes, she sounded as if she didn't know what I was talking about at first. Then, she told me that she had dropped them off."

"Drew, do you trust her?"

"I don't know. This was a little weird."

"Maybe it's your medicine. Why don't you lie down, and get some rest? Then, call her."

"I'll call her around her lunchtime."

"Good idea. Well, I have to go in. I'll chat with you later."

"Okay."

Salida went to work. She knew that everyone would have questions when she returned with a ring on her finger. She wanted to share the story of how she went to the clubhouse with Drew, how he proposed, and his family. Getting any work done would be almost impossible.

Salida's co-worker, Chelsea, was the first one to notice her ring.

"Get out! Really, he proposed?"

"Yes." Salida said while showing off her ring.

"Dang! I've been dating the same guy for over two years now, and I can barely get him to tell me that he loves me."

Salida shrugged, "Maybe he doesn't feel that way right now. It takes some men longer to realize how they feel about you."

"Oh, now you're the relationship counselor?"

"I'm just saying."

"Well, congratulations!"

"Thanks!"

Chelsea walked out of Salida's office. She rushed to the restroom to cry. She was madly in love with her boyfriend, but he made marriage seem hopeless to her. She wiped the tears away, and hurried back to her office.

All day, co-workers were in and out of Salida's office, admiring the ring Drew had purchased for her. She loved the attention she was receiving. She could almost feel the envy in some of the other workers. She smiled all day, proud of Drew's little work of art.

While Salida worked, Drew decided that he would spend some time writing. It was something he had always desired to explore, but until now, he hadn't really started. He preferred writing down his ideas first. He didn't like coming home to work on a computer after he had been working on one all day. Because he didn't have to work and he couldn't spend much time on his feet, he considered it a great day to start. He wrote until he had fallen asleep.

Weeks had gone by. Drew prepared himself to go with Salida to her hometown for Christmas to meet her mother. He was so excited that he was no longer on crutches, but wearing a boot didn't make things any better.
　　Drew hated shopping, but he wanted to purchase gifts for Salida and her mom. He wasn't exactly sure what to buy, but he knew that walking throughout the mall would give him a few ideas. He saw a few outfits that he would love to see Salida in, but he wasn't sure that she would agree on them. So, he purchased three gift cards from different stores. He also found a nice jewelry set for Salida and her mother. Drew was horrible at wrapping. Luckily, the jeweler wrapped the boxes. He also purchased a perfume set. He noticed the same perfume sitting on her dresser, and loved the smell of it. He, then, stopped by a store that sold lingerie. He thought that Christmas would be a great time for them to get closer. After buying the lingerie, Drew decided that he had purchased enough, and headed home.

Drew decided that he wanted to do something really special to set the mood for his and Salida's first time together. He made hotel reservations not far from her mother's house. Salida wanted to spend Christmas Eve at her mother's house as everyone enjoyed opening gifts early. So, the reservation was made for Christmas day.

On Christmas Eve, Salida called her mother to let her know that they were about to pull up to the house. Her sisters stood outside, waiting for the two of them to arrive. The look on their faces showed much approval when Drew stepped out of the car. They hurried over to hug her as they hadn't seen her all year. She lived less than two hours away from her hometown, but they never saw her. She visited her mother once every six months, only staying for a day or two. It wasn't always that way, but everyone knew why.

Drew choked as he entered the house. The smell of cigarettes filled the place.

"I forgot to tell you that my mom smokes."

"It's okay. I'm just not used to the smell."

With a cigarette in her hand, Salida's mom, Deanna, approached, "There's my baby!"

Salida wrapped her arms around her mom, squeezing tightly.

"You are looking really good now."

"Thanks, Mom. By the way, this is Drew, my fiancé."

"Did you say fiancé?"

"Yes ma'am."

Salida's mother turned to Drew, "Hi, I'm Deanna."

Drew reached out, and hugged her. Then, he replied, "I'm Drew."

Startled by the hug, Deanna said, "So, how come I've never met this young man?"

"He proposed on Thanksgiving day. I thought that today would be a great day to tell you that I was getting married."

Her mom looked down at Salida's hand, "Damn! Is that the ring he bought?"

"Yes." Salida held out her hand. Her sisters and mom crowded around the ring.

Drew stepped back. He noticed that her mom was a pro smoker. She could talk with the cigarette in her mouth. The smoke made him dizzy.

"What do you do for a living young man?"

"I reconcile accounts."

"That's a really nice ring!"

"Thank you!"

"Why don't you all come in here and have a seat?"

Drew asked, "Is it okay if I step outside for a minute?"

Everyone looked puzzled.

"I'm not used to the smell of smoke. It's making me a little dizzy."

"Oh, I'm sorry. I don't smoke a whole lot, not like I used to anyway. I'll smoke outside while you're here."

"This is your house. I can't stop you from smoking inside. I just need some fresh air. It's fine."

Drew stepped outside. Salida's mom put out her cigarette. "Is he serious?"

Salida replied, "Yes. He choked when he walked in. I asked you to stop smoking. Did you ever use that patch I had sent you?"
"No."
"The gum?"
"No."
"Mom, you have to stop smoking. Everyone can't take that smell. Obviously, he can't."
"I bet you he done smoked some weed or something before."
"I don't think he has. His family is very different from ours."
"What does that mean?"
"I mean that not all black families are the same."
"So, he came from some uppity family?"
"No, just a little more inviting. By the way, he's from the country."
"Oh. Well, people in the country smoke too."
Salida threw her hands up, "Just forget it."
"How did you meet him?"
"We met in a grocery store. He can really cook. I'll try to get him to make breakfast in the morning."
"How can you ask our guest to make breakfast for us in the morning?"
"I think he would love to make breakfast."
"Okay, we'll see."
Salida's mom looked out of the window to check on Drew.
"What happened to his foot?"
"He broke it playing basketball when we were in his hometown for Thanksgiving."
"Was he trying to show off?"
"No, it was his opponents fault."
"Okay," Deanna shrugged, while stepping away from the window.

When Drew returned, Salida showed him to his room. He closed the door behind himself, and let up the window. He thought to himself *luckily, she doesn't have roaches too.*
He lied back on the bed. He could tell that the sheets had been washed, but the stench from the cigarettes still engulfed the fresh smell. He sighed.
The cold air caused him to shiver, but he couldn't take the cigarette smell. He kept telling himself that it was only one night, one horrible night of sleeping in a cold room with his foot elevated, and enough clothes on for three people.

Salida and her family sat in the living room, watching television. Her brothers had returned from shopping along with her older sister's husband. "Is he going to ever come out of there? It's disrespectful to lock yourself in a room when you're the guest," said Deanna.

"He will. He just has to adapt to the smell."

"I think the window is up in that room. I walked past the room, and I could feel the cold air on my feet."

"I think he did too. He's just not used to the smoke."

"Where's Jon?"

"Momma, you can't talk to me about Jon, after I just introduced you to the man that I am going to marry!"

"I'm going to always love Jon no matter who you marry. He sure as hell didn't have a problem sitting in my house."

"That's because Jon grew up around smokers."

"Where is he?"

"I don't know. Home, I guess."

Salida's family laughed as her mom continued to pester her about her ex-husband.

Thirty minutes later, Drew entered the living room.

"The dead has risen," exclaimed Salida's mother.

Drew chuckled and coughed, "I'm sorry. I have asthma, and my parents didn't smoke. It takes some getting used to."

"Did you bring your inhaler?"

"Yes ma'am, but my asthma doesn't act up often. I hardly ever need one."

"I won't smoke in the house at all while you are here, okay?"

"It's okay. I didn't come here to change the way you do things. I'm just a visitor."

"Yeah, but I have to make you comfortable too. I'll stop."

Drew sat down beside Salida. Salida pointed in the direction of her brothers.

"Drew these are my brothers, Jason and Michael, and this is my sister's husband, Marcus."

Drew stood to shake hands with the other men in the room.

Salida added, "Hey, I told my family that you can cook."

He looked around the room as if responding to everyone, "I'm okay."

"Well, I was going to see if maybe we could go and get some breakfast tonight to cook in the morning."

Drew agreed, "That's fine with me... We should probably head out now. I'm sure the stores are closing early."

"Okay, let's go."

Drew and Salida headed out. As he drove he thought of how many people were in the house.

"Where is everyone going to sleep?"

"What do you mean?"

"There are a lot of people in the house. Where is everyone going to sleep?"

"My brother, Michael, lives on the same street. So, he's going to stay home, and come over early in the morning. There are three bedrooms upstairs, and two in the basement. The kids are going to sleep downstairs in the recreational room. My brother and his wife will take one bedroom downstairs. My sister and her husband will take the other."

"Oh, okay."

"Yeah, there's enough room. I didn't want to sleep downstairs because the kids are loud. You wouldn't get any sleep."

Drew wasn't as worried about the noise as much as he was worried about the cigarette smoke. He decided to take up as much time buying groceries as he possibly could. He decided to purchase hickory smoked bacon, thinking the bacon smell would overwhelm the smell of the smoke in the house. He also decided to purchase cough drops, air freshener, long johns, and an extra quilt. He knew he would have to heavily wrap the two of them to make it through the night. Salida laughed when she saw what he had purchased.

Drew was exhausted when they returned. Salida put up the groceries as Drew showered.

Drew's head ached as he stepped out of the shower. He applied lotion to himself, and stepped into his boxers, a pair of long john's, and a pair of sleeping pants. He also wore an undershirt, a t-shirt, and a thermal. Afterwards, he jumped into bed, longing for the next night.

Salida stayed in the living room, talking to the family. Drew's condition seemed to have worsened. Everyone could hear him coughing.

Frustrated with the coughing, Deanna said, "You better go and check on him. If he keeps coughing like that, you may not have anyone to marry."

The whole family laughed.

Salida replied, "He's okay. He's trying to sleep."

"He sounds horrible! Why is he coughing so much?"

"It's the smoke!"

"He's a wimp!"

"He's not. He's just not used to the smoke."

"Well, I haven't smoked in this house since he got here."

"Yes, but the house still smells like it. He's not used to it."

"How are you going to marry somebody that can't even be around me?"

"Mom, stop."

"I'm just saying. I saw that quilt he brought in. Is my quilt not good enough?"

"You're taking it the wrong way. He told you that he has asthma. When you smoke in the house, everything in the house smells like it."

"I just washed those quilts!"

"Yes, and they still smell like it. Keep your voice down, please."

"What? This is my house! I don't have to keep my voice down!"

"Mom, Drew is really trying to sleep, and you're trying to be difficult."

Deanna rolled her eyes, but said nothing. She knew Salida was right, but she enjoyed being the center of attention, even if she was perceived as being arrogant.

The next morning everyone awakened to the smell of bacon. Drew was just about finished cooking breakfast. The table was set, and fresh fruit was placed in the center. Deanna was impressed. Before everyone began to eat, Drew asked everyone to join hands so that he could bless the food. His prayer was short, but coveted by the other men of the house. After finishing his prayer in Jesus' name, everyone began to dig in.

Drew had also made hot chocolate for the kids, using his family recipe. The adults noticed that the kids were returning for seconds, and desired a cup of their own.

"Drew, this breakfast is amazing," exclaimed Deanna.

"Thank you!"

"Do you cook like that for Salida?"

"Only when she stays over to my place, or vice versa."

"Oh, really? So, you two have stayed over to each other's place."

Salida decided to join in on the conversation. "Yes, we have."

"Drew, have you taken any culinary classes," asked Salida's brother.

"I have. I can actually return to college, and get a degree within a year."

"Why don't you go back? This food is really good."

"I will. I haven't been as focused as I need to be. So, I don't feel as if I will obligate myself as much as I should. In due time, I will."

"Salida, you better put it down on him. A man that can cook like that is very rare. If he finishes school, and starts his own restaurant, the women will swarm around him like bees," advised her mother.

Drew chuckled, "That's not a problem. When I'm with someone, I'm with them. If I have asked for her hand in marriage, believe me, no woman can come between that. I read my Bible."

Deanna agreed, "I believe that. Your blessing over the food sent chills through me."

Everyone nodded their head in agreement. Salida smiled on the inside.

Everyone except Drew had eaten so much that they were sleepy again. They all decided to open their gifts, and return to bed. Drew pulled Salida to the side.

"Is it okay if I go for a walk through the neighborhood? I need to get some fresh air."

"Yeah, do you want me to go with you?"

"Not if you're full."

"Then, I can't go. I did overeat a little. Plus, I drank some of the hot chocolate.... You've never made that for me."

"I know. I usually make it when we're serving food to the kids at church."

"Oh, it was really good. We even ran out of it."

"I know. I could have made some more, but they wouldn't have eaten the other food if I did."

"That's true."

"By the way, I need to get the gift for your mother out of the trunk."

"You bought my mom a gift?"

"Of course I did."

"She's not expecting one from you."

"It's okay."

Drew headed to the car to get the jewelry set he had purchased for Salida's mother. He left Salida's gifts in the car so that he could give them to her that night.

After everyone had finished unwrapping gifts, Drew said, "I have one more!" He handed a small box to Salida's mother. She began to open it. She assumed that it was a small pendant of some sort, but to her dismay, he had purchased a beautiful necklace with matching earrings. Her eyes lit up as if it were the fourth of July.

"Oh my gosh! This is really nice!" She wrapped her arms around Drew. "Thank you so much! This is beautiful! I almost don't want to take it."

Drew smiled, "It's not a problem. I didn't want to come here empty-handed."

Salida's other siblings stepped closer to get a glimpse of the necklace. It was beautiful. Her brother, Jason, shook his head in amazement. Salida continued smiling on the inside. She knew that Drew was going to continuously amaze her family.

Drew stepped away to wash dishes. He wanted to finish the dishes, take a shower, pack his clothes, and check into the hotel. He figured that he could get some exercise at the fitness center there.

Deanna walked into the kitchen. "I really appreciate the necklace you purchased. I don't think anyone has ever purchased something like that for me."

"It's no problem. Salida means a lot to me. Therefore, her family means just as much. I want the best for her. I know that she's been through a lot, some things she's not even willing to share. I'm not here to hurt her. I'm here to help."

Deanna smiled, "Well, God bless you. I really underestimated you. I just want to apologize."

"There's no need. You should never give a man one hundred percent of you until you find that they're giving it back."

"I like that concept. I'll keep that in mind."

"Okay."

Drew continued washing the dishes. Deanna turned back, "You really shouldn't be in here, washing these dishes after you cooked the food."

"It's okay. I don't get to cook often. So, when I get the chance, I don't mind cleaning up my mess."

Deanna was overly impressed with Drew. She walked past Salida, "I don't know where in the hell you found him, but please find another one for me." Everyone laughed. Drew closed his eyes and shook his head, trying to hold in his own laughter.

Drew continued to wash the dishes, while everyone returned to their bed. He decided against walking in the neighborhood as he was afraid that he wouldn't be able to find the house when returning from the walk.

Drew and Salida checked into the hotel at three o'clock on the dot. He placed the bags and gifts in a closet. Salida was bowled over by the room. She wanted to rip Drew's clothes from him immediately, but she knew that he wouldn't allow it.

"I didn't go walking through your mom's neighborhood. I just jumped in the shower, and got ready. Do you want to work out in the fitness center here?"

Drew looked better, but sounded horrible.

Salida asked, "Are you getting sick?"

"Probably, sleeping in a cold room can do that to you. It's okay. I'm just glad I'll have some heat tonight."

Salida felt horrible. "I'm so sorry!"

"It's fine. I'm going to work out. I'll try to sweat some of this off of me."

"Go ahead. I might come down there. I'm still a little sleepy from being up all night, wrapping gifts with my mom."

"That's fine. You get some rest. We'll grab something to eat around five or so."

"Okay."

Drew headed to the fitness center, while Salida lied down. Before she fell asleep, she decided to check her messages.

She had received a "Merry Christmas" text from Jonathan. Because Drew had gone to work out, she replied.

Another text came through: So, what did ur mom say about ur fiancé? She called him a wimp: Salida replied.

He replied: LOL, I told u.

Salida laughed. Fifteen minutes later, the two of them were still texting each other, promising to meet so that they could exchange gifts. Eventually, Salida turned off her phone, and fell asleep.

Drew returned from the fitness center an hour later. He didn't want to spend too much time away from Salida. He entered the room and noticed that she was still sleeping. He rubbed her back to awaken her. She rolled over.

"Hey Babe, do you want to order in or go out to eat?"

"We can go out. Can you give me about thirty more minutes?"

"Sure, take as long as you want. I can wait. I'm going to shower while you are sleeping."

"Okay."

As soon as Drew returned from the shower, Salida awakened. She watched as he began to apply lotion. "Do you need some help?"

He turned, "I thought you were still sleeping."

"I'm up now!"

Drew laughed. He wanted to play along, but his plans were to eat, give her the gifts, and entertain her later. He turned his back to her.

Salida was frustrated. She shook her head, thinking that Jasmine might have been right after all. She stood, "I'm going to brush my teeth. Are we leaving at five?"

"We can leave at five. It's about fifteen 'til five now."

"Okay."

Ten minutes later, Drew was dressed, and ready to head out. His cologne was mesmerizing. Salida walked over to him.

"You smell so good."

"Thanks."

She planted light kisses on his lips. Drew returned the favor. Salida began to rub her hands up Drew's back, but his stomach started growling. Drew chuckled. "I need to eat. I didn't have much for breakfast."

Salida pouted, "Okay, okay, let's go."

The two of them headed out. Drew had checked on restaurants in the town. All of the nice ones were fifteen to twenty miles away. Salida was becoming impatient. "Drew, where are we going?"

"We're going to grab a bite to eat."

"Where?"

"Be patient. We're almost there."

Drew pulled up to the restaurant. He parked, and walked to her side to open the door.

"This is a really nice restaurant. I'm not dressed for this!"

"I'm dressed the same way you are. What does it matter to them?"

"Drew, you should have told me that we were coming here!"

"Calm down. It's okay. We're just going to eat."

Drew held out his hand for Salida. Hesitantly, she grabbed his hand. He escorted her into the restaurant, and pushed up her chair after they were seated. He looked in her direction, smiling as if she were the only person in the room. She blushed. "Sometimes I don't understand you, but you sure know how to take away everything that worries me."

"Told you Babe, they don't care what we're wearing, as long as we can afford the food."

The dinner was beyond belief. Every bite made them melt. Drew ordered dessert to take with them.

Salida settled into the car, "That food was so good! I can't believe I used to live here, and never went to that restaurant."

Drew smiled, "I'm glad you enjoyed it."

"I absolutely did!"

"Good, you can have the dessert whenever you're ready."

Salida wanted to reply to the dessert comment, but held her ground.

When they returned to the room, Drew walked to the closet to grab the gifts. "I've been waiting to give these to you all day."

Tears began to flow from Salida's eyes.

"What's wrong?"

She couldn't tell him that she hadn't been faithful. Nor could she tell him that only a few hours ago, she was making plans with her ex-husband. Instead, she sat shaking her head. Drew handed a box to her. She opened the box with the jewelry set.

"Drew, I can't take this. This is too much, the hotel, the dinner, the jewelry for my mom, now this? I can't."

"Salida, this is nothing in comparison to what I want you to have."

She smiled, and leaped towards him. "Thank you! Thank you! Thank you!"

He pushed her back, "We're not finished!" He handed her another box. This time, it was the lingerie, but Drew had sat the perfume set on top of it.

"Oh my gosh! How do you know that I wear this?"

"I saw it on your dresser."

"I love the lingerie! I would put it on for you, but I have to wash it first." Drew laughed, "I know."

"Thank you so much, Drew!"

He, then, handed her the gift cards. "I saw a few outfits in the mall that I would love to see you in, but I wasn't sure if you would like them. So, I just grabbed some gift cards."

Tears flowed even harder as she wrapped her arms around Drew. "You've done so much for me!" She pulled herself away to face him. "I got you something too."

"You did?"

"Yes, I did!"

Salida ran to the closet. "I hope you didn't think I just packed a lot of stuff in my bag."

Drew laughed. He was curious to find out what she had purchased for him. She brought three boxes back to the bed. Drew didn't open the boxes, instead he grabbed her, pulling her close. He wrapped his hands around her waist. "I wasn't finished."

"What do you mean," Salida asked.

"I have another gift to give you."

He rolled himself over her. Salida gasped for breath. She was so excited that he was finally giving her the gift she had been waiting for.

Salida sat in bed, not believing what had just happened. She bit her bottom lip; thinking of the way Drew had made her feel. She was so proud of him.

So many emotions flowed through her head. The sensation remained, causing her body to shiver slightly.

"Drew?" She waited for an answer. "Drew?"

"Yeah babe?"

"I'm cold."

"Okay, come here." He wrapped the cover around both of them. She was so close; she could feel his gift against her. She laid her head on his chest, rubbing her hand over it as if she was trying to get comfortable. Desiring that same sensation Drew had given her only minutes ago; she planted kisses on his chest. Drew rose to the occasion, giving her everything that she desired.

The following day, they slept until ten. Realizing that checkout was nearing, Drew jumped in the shower. He wanted to give Salida a little while longer to rest.

Salida jumped up while Drew was in the shower. She text her mother, sisters, and Chelsea: Uhmm, uhmmm, uhmmmm!

Chelsea text back: REALLY!!!

Salida replied: YESSSSSSSSS!!!!

Another text came in from Chelsea: OMG! I'm so jealous!!!

Salida closed with: We'll talk about it when I get back.

Salida turned her phone off, and waited for Drew to return from the shower. She hated that they had to leave.

Drew dreaded going back to Deanna's smoke-infested house, but he knew they would have to return to say their good-byes. Everyone was there, waiting on the two of them to return. Salida's sisters smiled as Drew walked into the house. Her mom turned her back as she pretended to busy herself. She chuckled slightly. Drew walked to the living room to shake hands with all of the men while Salida stayed in the kitchen with the women.

"You little slut, you are really glowing!" exclaimed Deanna.

"I'm just happy! What's wrong with that?" Salida replied with a grimace.

"I read your text."

Salida laughed, showing every tooth in her mouth, "I know!"

"I can't believe you told me that!"

"I couldn't help it! I couldn't hold it in!"

All of the women in the kitchen laughed.

Drew sat in the living room with the rest of the men, waiting for Salida. He noticed that her mom had placed plug-ins in the living room and hallway.

Where were those two days ago, he thought. He said nothing as the other men chatted away about their plans for the following year. Although the plug-ins were working, Drew felt a slight pounding in his head. He was ready to leave. He began to text Tamara as everyone chatted away.
Drew text: MERRY CHIRSTMAS!!!
Tamara replied: Same to you! How was it with her family?
Drew replied: I'll call to talk to you about it later. We have quite a bit to discuss.
She replied: Hope it's all good. You're getting married in six months.
He replied: I'll be ready. Chat w/u later!
He returned his phone to his side.

Salida entered the living room, "Are you ready?"
"Yeah, I'm ready."
"Okay, let's go."
Salida hugged everyone. Drew shook hands with the men, and hugged all of the women. Afterwards, the two of them headed home.

"Did you enjoy yourself?" asked Salida.
"I did enjoy myself. You have a beautiful family."
"Yes, they are beautiful."
"Your mom is a trip. I wasn't expecting her to be that way. I was thinking a little more conservative, almost snobby."
"Why?"
"Because you come off as conservative, but it seems natural."
"Are you calling me snobby?"
"No, I said conservative. Your mom is very laid back, but she enjoys attention. She's also that my-way-or-no-way kind of person."
"I'll agree with that."
Drew said nothing more. He knew he was on the verge of upsetting Salida.
"So, what did you think of my siblings?"
"All of them were really cool. Your sisters are undeniably beautiful."
Salida had always felt as if she wasn't as attractive as her other sisters. A hint of jealousy kicked in after Drew made the comment.
"So, you were checking out my sisters?"
"Not like that. I have the sister that I plan to marry. I'm just saying that no one could ever tell them that they aren't attractive."
Salida shrugged, "I guess." She tried to kill the attraction before it started. "They're just a little different."

"Everybody is different. Even my sisters aren't the same. Chrissy is a little more hard core, always ready to fight. Ree, or Gloria, is extremely generous and caring, and Flo is laid back."

"My older sister cheats on her husband. My younger sister can't find a husband to cheat on. Every guy that she dates is a loser."

"Everybody makes bad choices at some points in time. Nobody is perfect. Let them figure it out. We can't help by negating them. They're your sisters. Love them no matter what decisions they make."

Salida folded her arms in frustration. Drew turned up the music, not wanting to discuss Salida's family as he realized that she didn't quite agree. For an hour, they rode in silence. Then, Salida asked, "Did you open your gifts?"

"I opened one." Drew held out his arm. "See, I'm wearing the sweater you purchased."

She wanted to smack herself. It was actually the sweater she had purchased Jonathan. "Oh, it looks really nice on you!" She thought to herself, *Jon wouldn't have been able to wear it anyway. His arms are larger.*

"Thanks! I really like it!"

She smiled, "You're welcome!"

She sat, wondering if she had given Drew another gift that she meant to purchase for Jonathan. She would have been really upset with herself if she gave Drew the watch she had purchased. Jonathan always went out of his way to purchase nice gifts for Salida. She wanted to return the favor. Drew's gifts were great, but she knew he was no match for Jonathan.

When the two of them made it back, Drew immediately changed clothes and fell across his bed. He tossed the clothes that he had worn back in the hamper as there was a hint of smoke still lingering on them. Salida walked into the room. "I have to unpack, and get ready for work tomorrow."

"You have to work tomorrow?"

"I told my boss that I would come in for a few hours tomorrow."

"Oh, okay... I was hoping that we could spend a little more time together since the day is still young."

"I wish we could too, but I really have to unpack, shower, and get some rest. I'm going in early. I know I have a lot of paperwork on my desk."

"I understand." Drew stood to hug Salida. She hugged him back, but seemed distant. He looked at her.

"What's wrong with you?"

"Nothing."

"There's something wrong. You've never hugged me that way."

"Well, I didn't like the comment you made about my sisters."

"I only said that they were beautiful! Nothing more! Would you have been okay if I said they were ugly?"

"I wouldn't have believed you if you said that."

"So, what's wrong with me complimenting your family?"

"It's not that you complimented them, it's how you complimented them." Drew was bewildered. "Salida, what is the problem with you and your sisters?"

"There's not a problem."

"Obviously, there is. I complimented them, and you're upset about it. Let's just pretend that I never said it."

"I can't do that. I'm not the oldest or the youngest. I'm just the one in the middle, the only one that lost someone very dear to her, and the only one that has been divorced. You don't think that bothers me?"

"Maybe, but that doesn't make me love you any less." Drew pointed towards the bed, "Please sit." He shook his head. "You and your sisters will never live the same life. God never intended for you all to go through the same things. That's what makes us all unique. There are going to be some things that you will go through that they could never handle, and vice versa. What matters is that He loves you all the same. Your mom does too. She also knows which ones need more attention than others. All of you are beautiful girls, but you are the one that God has chosen for me. I could never feel about either of them the way that I feel about you. I can promise you that. I love everything about you."

Salida smiled.

Drew continued, "Honestly, I don't even know why we're having this conversation. When I put that ring on your finger, I knew that you were the one I wanted to spend the rest of my life with."

"Drew, I'm sorry. I'm really sorry." Salida shook her head. "Maybe, I'm just tired."

"You can lie down with me for a while."

"I can't. I really need to unpack, and get ready for tomorrow." She stood. "I know that you aren't attracted to my sisters. And you're right, there are some things that I have gone through that they could never handle." She hugged Drew. "I'll call you tomorrow on my way to work."

"Okay, Babe. I love you."

"I love you too."

Drew kissed Salida's forehead as she seemed hesitant about kissing his lips. Afterwards, she left.

Salida called Jon as soon as she left Drew's driveway.

"You're late!"

"I'm on my way. Drew started chatting when we got back. I tried to even accuse him of having a crush on my sisters to have a reason to leave."

"Why would you do that?"

"I don't know. I didn't want him to feel as if he had to go overboard to prove me wrong. So, I just told him that I was tired."

"Of all of the things you could think of to leave, accusing him of checking out your sisters is insane."

"Okay, I get it!"

"So, do you have to change clothes?"

"I have on a skirt, and fitted shirt. Is that okay?"

"That's fine. I'm sure you look nice."

Salida applied makeup as she headed in Jonathan's direction.

"So, where are we going?"

"You know that I never tell what I have up my sleeves."

Salida grimaced. Jonathan always knew how to excite her. She checked her makeup again, when she arrived.

The door was already opened for her to enter. As Salida walked in, Jonathan handed her a box. "I was supposed to give this to you later, but it's perfect for you to wear tonight."

Salida's dress was breath-taking. The earrings, necklace, and shoes that Jonathan also purchased made it look even better. She felt like a jewel. She stood in the mirror, admiring her reflection.

"I love it!"

"I told you that he doesn't know you."

"Jon, let's not talk about him right now."

Jonathan held out his arm for Salida as they headed to the show.

After the show, the two of them headed to the hotel. When Salida entered the hotel room, a trail of roses engulfed the place along with a bottle of champagne and truffles. Salida turned to Jonathan. She was so ready for him. Jonathan pulled her close. "I wasn't sure if you wanted to eat out or not. I ordered room service while we were at the show, but if you don't want to eat here, we don't have to."

Salida shook her head. "Here is fine."

He pulled up the chair for her to sit. Salida was mesmerized. He, then, pulled up a chair beside her, and rubbed his fingers through her hair.

"Do you know how much I love you?"

She looked into his eyes, "I do."

"So, why are you doing this to me? It drives me crazy knowing that you are six months away from marrying someone else."

"I know, Jon. I really shouldn't have gotten involved with Drew, but I didn't think it would go this far. However, I do care a lot about him. He's different."

"He's very different. He's a wimp. That man has no balls. I would have knocked a man out if he ruined my meal with my girl. When you told him to sit down, he did nothing."

"He's not a fighter... I thought I told you that I didn't want to talk about him."

"Okay, but it's really hard for me to see you with him like that."

"I'm sorry. I'll figure something out."

"Did you sleep with him when you were home?"

Salida held her head down, "You can't ask me that."

"Did you?"

"Jon."

"You did."

"I... what was I supposed to do? We were at the hotel, and..."

Jonathan shook his head, "Spare the details." He stood to walk away. He tightened his fists. "Damn it!"

Salida stood, and walked over to Jonathan. "I'm sorry Jon.... I'm so sorry."

Tears rolled from Jonathan's eyes, "This would have never happened if we didn't lose our son! Salida, we were happy. We were happy as a family. I know that I should have never walked away from you. I left you vulnerable, available to any man. I should have never done that. Now that I want to make things right, it's too late. I blamed you for something you had no control over. I was angry with you, angry with God, just angry." He wrapped his arms around her as they both wept, "I'm sorry. I really want to make this right, but I don't know what to do."

For a moment they both sat, holding each other. Salida pushed away, and turned her back to Jonathan. "I need to shower. I feel filthy after sleeping with Drew." She shook her head. "Now, I'm here at this hotel with you." She turned to Jonathan. "What kind of woman am I becoming? I have brought someone else into my life. I agreed to marry him. Now, I'm sitting at this hotel with my ex-husband."

Jonathan grabbed her, examining her face as if checking her soul, "Listen, I can't find fault with you. I was the one that walked away. We're going to make this right. Okay?"

"Okay."

Salida showered while Jonathan laid out the gifts that he had purchased for her. When she stepped out of the shower, she shook her head. "Jon, I can't take those gifts."

"You have to. These are gifts that represent every year that we have been apart. I owe that to you."

"You don't owe me anything."

"Please, just take them."

"I can't. I'll feel like some money hungry slut."

"Lida, I'm not asking you for anything. Just take what I'm giving."

Salida sat on the bed, and Jonathan began to apply lotion to her body. "Jon, I know that you've always done this for me, but I feel horrible. I've allowed another man to touch me, to enter me. I gave to him what belongs to you."

Jonathan's head fell, "I know, Babe. I really don't want to even think about it."

"Can we not have sex tonight? Less than twenty-four hours ago, I shared myself with someone else."

Jonathan agreed, "That's fine. Let's get some rest."

Jonathan removed the wrapped gifts from the bed, and placed them in a chair by the bed. He, then, began to remove his clothes. Salida jumped into bed, and turned her back to him.

"What's wrong?"

"I can't watch."

He smirked, "You're a mess."

She agreed, "I know. I've never been able to resist you. Tonight, I'm struggling."

"I'll leave on my shirt and boxers."

"That doesn't keep me from wanting you."

"Then, I'll sleep in the chair."

"No. Please, don't do that."

"What do you want me to do?"

Salida cried, hating herself for sleeping with Drew. "Just hold me, Jon. Hold me like you've always held me."

He entered the bed, watching her, realizing she was waiting for him. He wrapped his arms around her. "Hey?"

"Yes?"

He planted a kiss on the back of her head. "I won't let you do anything tonight. I promise."

"That's not fair for you!"

"It's okay... It's okay. I'm here."

Jonathan and Salida slept. He held her all night, and into the morning.

That morning, after leaving the hotel, Salida headed to work. She called Drew three minutes before she pulled into the parking lot.

"Good morning!"

Salida laughed as Drew seemed to have been singing. She replied, "Good morning."

"Did you rest okay?"

"I did. How about you?"

"I did. I wished that you were here."

"Did you?"

"Yes."

She wasn't sure what to say.

He asked, "Do you want to grab lunch later?"

"Umm... I'm not sure. It depends on how busy I am. If not, I'll stop by to see you."

"Okay."

"Well, I'm pulling up to the dealership now. I'm a little early, but I wanted to hurry up and get here so that I can finish early. I'll call you when I leave."

"Alright, I'll talk to you later."

Salida turned off her phone, and sighed. She sat in her car, thinking of how she could end her engagement. She knew that it would hurt Drew. The thought of hurting him sickened her. Their relationship was perfect until Jonathan came back in the picture.

Salida's heart had always melted for Jonathan. She knew that she could never love Drew as much. She rubbed her hands over her face, frustrated and angry with herself. Her desire for Jonathan was extreme. It took everything out of her to not touch him the previous night. Anxiety began to kick in as she sat in her car. She realized that she couldn't trust her own judgment. She decided that she would pray.

"God help me, please. I have never been through anything like this. Drew is a really good guy. He's family oriented, handsome, humble... an amazing prayer. It seems like when he's praying he knows you're going to do what he asks of you. His faith in you is beyond belief. His prayers make everyone's spirit rise. He's also reliable. That man can make any woman submissive because he's sure to do his part.

Jonathan has some of those qualities, but not as strong. He also has this confidence about himself that makes him seem arrogant as times, but that same confidence makes me love him more. He knows it. He has to feel it."

She laid her head on the steering wheel.

"God, I don't know what to do. I'm a mental mess. Please help me to make the best choice for myself. In Jesus' name I pray, amen."

She opened the door to step out of her car, and headed towards the office. She made a stop in the break room after deciding to grab some coffee to cure the sleep that still lingered.

She sat in her office, typing away, but considering her options. She was certain that she wanted to work things out with Jonathan. He was too much of right for her. He knew everything about her; every expression, everything that bothered her, her family, her flaws, everything. She looked down at the ring she wore, shaking her head as it reassured her that she belonged to someone else. She decided to inform Drew that they should wait until they're married to sleep together again.

Salida text Drew around noon: Hey! I hope your day is going okay. I wanted 2 discuss something w/u.

Drew replied: K. R u coming over, or u want 2 meet?

She replied: I'll come over after work.

She sat her phone down, and continued working, deciding to leave around two o'clock as she was almost finished with all of her paperwork.

Drew was asleep on the couch, when Salida knocked on the door. He slept off and on all day after taking different medications. He stood to walk to the door. He felt very light-headed.

"Good afternoon," Salida said as he opened the door.

"Good afternoon. How was work?"

"It was great! I got a lot done."

"That's good."

Salida noticed that Drew seemed a little out of it. "Are you okay?"

"I'm okay."

"You don't look like you're okay."

"I feel a little dizzy, but I just woke up."

"Have you eaten?"

"I ate a little this morning. I'm not really hungry right now."

"What's wrong?"

"My asthma was acting up a little, but I'll be okay."

"Oh."

Drew pulled Salida closer to him, wanting to reassure her that he desired her, but she pushed away.

"Drew, I need to talk to you."

"Okay, let's sit."

They headed to his living room to sit on the couch. He watched as she struggled to get her words together.

"Is something wrong?"

"Well, we're getting married in June, and I was thinking that maybe we should wait until then to have sex again."

"Babe, that's not a problem."

"Really?"

Drew humped in his shoulders, "It's not. Making love to you the other night was wonderful, but I can wait."

Salida struggled to shake off the thought of how Drew made her feel that night, "Yes, it was wonderful….and extremely fulfilling." She bit her lip, trying to fight the desire to tackle Drew at that very moment. "I have to go." She headed towards the door.

Confused, Drew said, "I thought you wanted to talk."

"I do, but…. I can't right now." She held her head down, not able to even face him. Drew was handsome, and awfully irresistible. Standing in front of her with only a tank top and boxers made the situation worse. "Please, put on some clothes."

Drew looked down at his attire, "Oh, I'm sorry." He headed to his room to grab his sweats and another shirt. Salida was behind him, aggression building in every step. He turned to her. "What are you doing?"

"Sorry." She pushed him to the bed. Drew was shocked.

"I thought you…"

"I know."

"We don't have to…"

Drew headed to the kitchen, while Salida slept. He thought to himself *she's a monster.* He decided that he would make something for both of them to eat, while she slept. He had an extra bottle of wine that would go perfect with the meal, but he decided against it. He continued cooking, adding seasoning when necessary.

Salida awakened to the smell of Drew's cooking. She took a deep breath as she considered what she had just done. She asked herself, "How come you can't control yourself? He even offered to put on some clothes, and you still couldn't get it together! What is wrong with you?" She shook her head, and rolled over; battling with her own demons.

A month had gone by, and Salida seemed to avoid Drew and Jonathan by wrapping herself in work. She stayed away from Jonathan because she had slept with Drew. She stayed away from Drew because she didn't trust herself in his presence. She made sure that she could only see him when they were in a public setting.

Salida also noticed that her cycle was overdue by two weeks. Fear had set in, but she was almost certain that it was only stress from working and worrying about whether or not she should marry Drew. She also feared the fact that Valentine's Day was only three weeks away, and she knew both men would want to be with her on that day. Salida wasn't sure what to do. She considered having a girl's night with some of her single co-workers. She also considered getting her siblings together to take her mother out to eat. She knew that Drew would definitely find a reason to not come with her. Her older brother would also find some excitement in not having to take his petty, nagging, rude, always wanting something wife out by himself. She sent a text to her siblings. All agreed to meet except her younger brother. He had something really special planned for his wife. Salida was excited. She was indecisive about where to take her mom, but she was sure that she would figure something out within the next three weeks.

On February 7th, Drew and Salida were sitting in an Italian restaurant when Salida announced that she was heading to her mother's for Valentine's Day. Drew was shocked at the thought of her driving to her hometown to take her mother out.

"So, when did you decide that you were going to go to your hometown for Valentine's Day?"

"There was a mass text that had gone out, asking all of the siblings to meet to take her out. We all agreed. So, I'm going to go home. I'm coming back the next day."

"That's fine." Drew sighed, "Well, I guess I'll stay here, and work."

Salida smirked. She knew her plan would work.

She was finishing her lasagna when the waiter walked by with a seafood dish for the guests sitting behind her. The aroma made Salida nauseous. She excused herself, and headed to the restroom. Although it wasn't a private restroom, Salida locked the door. She took the lid off of the garbage can just in time to relieve herself of everything she had eaten. She couldn't believe the aroma from the seafood was so intense. She grabbed paper towels to wipe her face. Then, she washed her mouth out. She also returned the top to the garbage can, and washed her hands. Afterwards, she returned to her seat.

"Are you okay," asked Drew.

"Yeah... yeah, I'm fine." She looked up at Drew. "Why'd you ask?"

"Because you made this weird face, and ran to the restroom."
"The seafood that the waitress brought over was so strong that it was unbearable!"
Drew frowned, "Oh."
The smell was returning, but it seemed even stronger as she sat. Drew watched in dismay. Ha advised, "How about we just get our food, and leave?"
Salida felt like more of her food was coming up. She nodded her approval, and excused herself again.
Drew sat with his head down, waiting on the waitress to bring carryout plates. When she returned with the plates, he handed her his credit card to cover the bill. He emptied their food into the plates, and waited for Salida to return. Salida returned just as the waitress handed Drew his card. Drew thanked the waitress, handed her a tip, and escorted Salida out of the restaurant.
For the first five minutes in the car, they sat in silence. Drew asked, "Have you started your period?"
Salida bit her bottom lip, "I'm a little late."
"How late are you?"
"A few weeks, a month maybe..."
"How come you haven't said anything about it?"
"What are you talking about?"
"Have you taken a test to see if you're pregnant?"
"No, I haven't... I'm not pregnant. I've been under a lot of stress lately. That delays my cycle sometimes."
"Are you in denial or something?"
Salida frowned, "What?"
Drew didn't respond. Instead, he pulled up to the closest convenient store, and grabbed a pregnancy test.
Frustrated, Salida asked, "Why did you buy that?"
"Because we're going to go to my house, and you're going to take the test."
"I'm not taking that test!"
"You are because I want to know."
"What is up with you? Did you not just hear me say that I'm not taking that test?"
Drew said nothing. He parked his car at his house, and opened the door for Salida.
Adamantly she said, "I want to go home."
"I'll take you home once you've taken the test."
"No, I want to go home now!"

Drew shook his head. "Salida, why are we arguing? You've had these crazy mood swings lately. You've also been avoiding me. I wasn't sure what was going on with you. You never come to the house. You used to be here almost daily. Now, the only time I get to see you is when we're meeting somewhere, when we need to get some groceries, or when we're exercising. I thought that maybe you were going through something that you didn't want to discuss. So, I kept my distance. Now, you're sitting in the car, trying to argue with me about taking a pregnancy test!" He opened the door wider. "Can you please come in the house and take the test? I just want to know for myself."

Salida stepped out of the car, and entered the house. Drew handed her the test.

"This is embarrassing!"

"How so? We're getting married in June, and you're afraid to take a pregnancy test?"

Salida huffed, "I'm going to take it!" She held up the test, "See, I'm headed to the bathroom now."

For twenty minutes, Salida sat on the bathroom floor with her head down. She wasn't sure how far along she was. She was certain that it wasn't Jonathan's. She hadn't slept with him since Thanksgiving, and had been on her cycle since then. Drew was another story. She covered her face with her hands, "God, please don't do this to me. What am I going to tell Jon? I was supposed to tell Drew that I'm not going to marry him next week. Now, I'm pregnant by him. What am I supposed to do?" Tears began to flow down her face.

Drew knocked on the door. "Are you okay?"

Salida wiped her face, "Yes." She unlocked the door for him to enter. When he saw her face, he knew the answer. He grabbed her, holding her tightly. "It's okay... it's okay."

"Drew, what are we going to do?"

"We're going to make an appointment with the doctor to see how far along you are. Then, we'll wait for our seed to grow."

"Are you sure you want a child with me? I've been mean and moody. I haven't been here like I'm supposed to."

"Do you want to be here?"

She didn't know what to say.

"Do you?"

"Drew, I love you. I love the time we spend together. I agreed to marry you." She shook her head. "I'm so confused right now. I wanted us to wait until we were married to sleep together again. Now, I'm pregnant. What's the point in waiting?"

Drew added, "You have been really mean to me lately, as if I'm doing something wrong. I thought that maybe I was overcrowding you. So, I decided to give you some space. Still, you don't call as much and small things agitate you..." Drew shook his head. "Things have been really different lately. What's wrong with you?"

Salida sat on the couch, "Drew, you're an amazing guy. You're extremely handsome, you have great work ethics, the moral and values of your family are beyond belief, you're a prayer warrior, any woman would go after you.... Salida pointed to herself, "Me, I don't feel as if I'm good enough."

Drew sat beside her, "Why do you feel that way?"

She shook her head, "Look at my family for one. We're nowhere near as close to God as your family. My mom has a relationship with God, but it's not like your mom's. I see the difference in our families. Plus, you have always had both parents in your life. I can't tell you where my father is."

Drew replied, "Not having your father in your life doesn't change what you value. God is always there to replace whoever isn't present. Our families are different, but that doesn't mean that we aren't compatible. Salida, we attend church together every Sunday. We're still building our relationship, and growing in the word of God. "

"That's true, but my relationship with God is not as strong as yours. You were okay with not sleeping with me. Even when I literally tackled you that night, you were hesitant. No man has ever waited on me like that. Right now, talking to you about the way you make me feel has my hormones in an uproar. I have tried to fight my demons. I've stayed away from you to suppress those things that build inside of me. I want you constantly." Salida began to glow as she expressed herself. Her fire was slowly igniting. "Every day, I want you to make me feel the way I felt the other times."

Drew hushed Salida. He considered everything that she had said to him. His relationship with God truly made a difference for him. Otherwise, he would have had his way with her. However, Salida's words made Drew realize that her heart wasn't for him. Therefore, he decided to take her home. "Let's go."

"Where are we going?"

"I'm taking you home."

Salida was confused. "I just told you that I'm pregnant, and desire to sleep with you. Why are you taking me home?"

"Because you never answered me when I asked if you wanted to be here. Instead, you gave me reasons as to why you don't feel as if you're good enough. My pastor always told me that if a person can state that they're not good enough, they're really not good enough."

"So, you're going to take me home?"

"Yes. You wanted to go home. I wanted you to take the test. Now, we know that you are pregnant."

"So, you're going to take me home, and that's it? Are you saying that you're not going to have anything to do with me?"

"No, that's not what I'm saying. Salida, I asked you to marry me. You agreed. That means that we both agreed to spend the rest of our life together. How can we do that, when you couldn't tell me that this is where you want to be? Instead, you keep giving me reasons as to why you have doubt. I love you. I've shown you nothing, but love. There's something going on in your life. I'm not sure what it is. I want to be with you, but don't stay for me. Stay because this is where you truly want to be." As he began to put on his coat, he added, "Another thing, I would never walk away from my child. Therefore, I'm going to be there. But, until you decide where you want to be, we can cancel the wedding." Drew held out his hand for the ring.

Salida sat with her head down. She slid the ring off of her finger, and handed it to him.

"Are you ready?"

She nodded. She knew that Drew was right.

The two of them sat in silence as he drove her to her house. She was hurt that Drew took the ring. The fact that he took it on the day that she found out she was pregnant bothered her even more. She weighed her options. She knew that Jonathan would be hesitant about taking her back after finding that she was pregnant by Drew. She debated on whether or not to tell him.

As Drew pulled up to the house, Salida opened the door, got out of the car, and went into her house without a word. He watched as the only woman he's ever loved so much pretended that he was a cab driver. He swallowed hard, wondering how she could be so cold. He called Tamara.

"Hello?"

"Tam?"

"Hey, Drew!"

"We need to talk."

"What's wrong?"

"Why'd you ask that?"

"I can hear it in your voice."

"Salida gave me back the ring."

"What?"

"She gave the ring back. I asked her if she wanted to be there. She never told me that she did. Instead she gave me reasons as to why I would be a great candidate for any other woman. When I held my hand out for the ring, she handed it to me."

"Did she even hesitate?"

"No, she just slid it off."

"Wow. Are you okay?"

"It hurts, but I'm glad that I know how she feels now. I was going to marry her in June." Drew continued, "When we first started dating, everything was perfect. I wanted things to stay that way. Things were never rocky between us. Since I proposed to her, things have been on the edge. She's had this attitude as if I get on her nerves. She stays away more. Before, we did so much together. Now, I hardly see her."

"Did you ask her about it?"

"She stated that she stayed away to keep herself from sleeping with me. I can understand that she was trying to wait. I'm okay with it. But her attitude has changed."

"That's not good. Drew, you're such a good guy."

"And she's pregnant."

"What?"

"She is. We found out today."

"Wait a minute! She found out she was pregnant, and she gave you back the ring in the same day?"

"Yes." Drew thought for a minute. Then, asked Tamara. "Do you think I was wrong for saying that we should cancel the wedding, after finding out that she was pregnant?"

"Drew, I don't know. I'm not one to give advice on relationships. You see how my relationships have been. Talk to your father."

"I can't talk to my father about Salida."

"Really? Why?"

Drew was reluctant about telling Tamara what his father thought. Instead, he made up an excuse. "My father and I don't really discuss relationships."

"Has he been hard on you about relationships or something?"

"Not really. He just gives suggestions."

"Well, are you taking heed to the suggestions?"

"I have." Drew wanted to change the subject, but had nothing else to talk about. "Hey, I'm going to call you back in a minute. I have to do something right now."

"Okay."

He hung up with Tamara, needing to give his brain a break.

In the meantime, Salida had called Jonathan.

"Hello?"

"Hey, what are you doing right now?"

"I'm not doing anything. You sound a little shaky?"

"What do you mean?"

"You sound as if something is bothering you. Are you okay?"

"Can you come over?"

"Yes. Give me twenty minutes, and I'll be there."

"Okay."

Salida wasn't sure about telling Jon that she was pregnant. However, she was excited to tell him that the wedding was off. She weighed her options. She knew that she would eventually have to tell him, but she wasn't sure that this would be a great time to do it. She cleaned the house a little as she waited for Jonathan. She knew there wasn't much to clean, but keeping herself busy took away the worry.

Jonathan arrived in no time. He startled Salida as he knocked on the door.

"Hey!" she said as she opened the door.

"Hey! How are you feeling?"

"I'm fine."

"So, what's wrong?"

"I gave Drew back the ring."

Jonathan smiled as he started to pick her up, and swing her around. Salida stopped him.

"What's wrong? Aren't you happy?"

She held her head down. "There's another problem."

Jonathan stood, waiting for Salida tell him.

She reached into her purse, and pulled out the pregnancy test that she had wrapped in plastic.

"Jonathan, I'm pregnant."

Jonathan smiled. He was so excited to hear of Salida's pregnancy. He grabbed her, wrapping his arms around her. Then, he realized that she was unwavering. He checked her expression. He asked, "By me?"

She shook her head, "No."

Jonathan pushed himself away from her, and headed towards the door.

Salida reached out for him, "Jon, please don't walk away from me."

"How could you be so careless?"

"Jon, please!"

"Do you really think I want to help you raise another man's child? Why did you even give the ring back? Now, you're stuck with him. He's going to be around for the rest of your life. What makes you think I want to have anything to do with that?"

"If you really love me like you say you do, this wouldn't stop us from being together!"

Jonathan was outraged. "I can't believe you called me over here to tell me this!" He looked at her as if she disgusted him. "You should have just told me over the phone." He walked out, slamming the door as he exited.

Salida sat on the couch, not believing Jonathan's reaction to her pregnancy. She wasn't sure how to respond as anger had replaced her sadness. She lay back on the couch, covering herself with the throw that hung over the side of the couch.

Salida went to her mother's for Valentine's Day. She hadn't told the family anything in regards to the wedding or her pregnancy. When she arrived, the family stood at the door, looking to see if Drew was on the passenger side. Her mother had placed plug-ins all over the house in preparation for his return. The whole family was startled to see that Salida was alone.

"Where's Drew?" her mother asked.

"He had to work."

"Oh!" Her mom stood, curiosity building as she realized that Salida had never come home for Valentine's Day. "You know, this is not really a holiday that you would come home to celebrate."

Salida replied, "I know. I just wanted to do something different this time."

Deanna noticed that the ring was gone, but didn't ask why. She knew Salida would give her a bogus reason as to why she didn't wear the ring. Instead, she walked away, wondering what had gone wrong to cause Salida to return the ring.

Everyone sat in the living room, watching television as they waited for the time to leave. Salida's sister grabbed her hand as she walked by, "Why aren't you wearing your ring?"

"It's getting cleaned."

"Oh. So, the wedding is still on?"

Salida looked around. She noticed that everyone was watching her, waiting for an answer. "Of course it is. You don't meet a man like that every day. I'd have to be crazy to walk out of his life."

Her mom replied, "That's true. He's a good man."

Salida was becoming nervous as everyone seemed to watch her every move. She text Drew when everyone had their heads glued to the television: Drew, I really miss you. Not having you here has been extremely horrible for me. Let's try to work this out.

Drew replied: Salida, I need to know that you really need me.

She replied: I do need you. Please, give me a chance to show you that. I'm sorry that I've been so mean to u. I'm pregnant with our child! My emotions have been running wild.

Drew replied: Okay, we can get together when you get back from your mother's. Give me a call.

She ended with: Okay.

Salida smiled. She knew that he was soft for her. Whether she was in love with him or not, she knew that he was going to be a great father and husband. With Jon walking out on her, she had to do something. Trying to work her hours, and raise a child alone seemed impossible to her.

The family headed out to the restaurant thirty minutes before they were supposed to be there. That would give them a five to ten minute wait time. Salida was extremely hungry, but didn't want anyone else to know. The aroma of the food made her even more impatient as they waited for a table. She sat in the waiting area, playing a game on her phone, trying to let the time pass without getting frustrated.

When they were seated, she ordered appetizers. Everyone else ordered alcoholic beverages. Her mother watched as she continued playing the game.

"Lida, are you not going to order a drink?"

"No ma'am. I'm just going to drink water, and I'll probably get a soda when my meal comes out."

"Are you hungry?"

Salida stopped playing the game to look at her mother, "I am... why are you watching me?"

Her mother shook her head, "Something is different about you."

Salida said nothing. She started playing her game again.

When the appetizers arrived, Salida advised that everyone was ready to order their meal.

"I'm not ready," her sister added.

"Me either," stated her older brother.

Salida placed the phone on the table. "What's taking you two so long? We've been here long enough for you to go over the menu." She looked at the waiter. "I'll go ahead and order while we are waiting on them."

After placing her order, Salida dug into the appetizer that was sitting on her table.

Deanna asked, "Are you going to pray over your food?"

"I did. I prayed alone."

"You're really hungry, huh?"

"I am." Salida sighed, "Please stop watching me. Maybe that's the reason I don't come here often."

"You're just out of pocket a little. You didn't get a drink, you're eating the appetizer as if you're the only person that was supposed to eat it, and you didn't wait to pray with the family."

She threw her hands up, "Sorry!" She looked around as everyone else stared at her in dismay.

Deanna prayed. Afterwards, everyone began to eat the appetizer at their table. Salida drank two refills of water while waiting on her food. Everyone became anxious as the food arrived. Salida was about to dig into her food, when the fish smell returned. She excused herself, and rushed to the restroom. She wasn't sure who ordered the fish. She only knew that the smell was overwhelming. She washed her mouth and hands, and returned to the table. Deanna sat at the table with her arms folded. She was certain that she knew what was wrong with Salida.

Salida knew that Deanna would find out. If anyone could ever figure out what was going on with their children, it would be Deanna. Salida nodded her head towards Deanna to reassure her that what she thought was true. She lifted her finger to her mouth to hush her. Deanna grimaced, but asked for a to-go plate as she was the one that ordered the fish. Salida thanked her quietly.

"Mom, you're not going to eat?" asked Salida's sister.

"I ate a little, but I want some dessert."

"Okay."

Salida sighed. She was relieved once the waiter took Deanna's food to the back to place it in a to-go box. Deanna played along as Salida finished most of her meal. Because she was unable to consume her dinner, she ate all of her dessert. However, it was well worth it.

As everyone began to finish their meals, Salida advised that she would head back home that night.

Deanna objected, "It's too late for you to be on the road, trying to get back home. You should stay, and leave in the morning."

Without hesitation, Salida agreed.

The next morning, before she left, she and Deanna sat in the kitchen, chatting about her plans for the next child. Deanna was curious to know how cooperative Drew would be and what is going to come of the two of them. She listened as Salida talked about how Drew would be a great father, how he was sure to handle things, and never walk away from the two of them. There was one other thing that she noticed. She asked, "So, where is your heart?"
"What do you mean?"
"You're not in love with Drew. I can tell."
She watched Salida's expressions. Salida could never look at Deanna when she was right about something.
"How can you tell something like that? I've never said anything negative about him!"
"I know, but all you've really said is that he's going to handle his business because he's that kind of man. It's not that you actually love him. You just know that he's a good man." Deanna shook her head. "It's sad to say, but I actually feel sorry for him."
"Why?"
"Because you're about to marry someone else's husband."
Salida sat with her head down. "Are you saying that I'm not good enough for Drew?"
"Absolutely not! I'm saying that you're only marrying him because you don't want to be alone." She watched Salida for a moment. "What are you going to do when the person that you're supposed to be with comes along?"
Salida finished the orange juice that she was drinking. She stood to hug Deanna. "Mom, I have to go. I'll call you to let you know when I've made it back."
Deanna kissed the side of Salida's face. "Love you."
"I love you too."

After work, Salida headed to Drew's. She thought of everything Deanna had said to her. She thought: *What does she know? She's not married. How can I take advice from a woman that's not even married? Is she waiting on someone to return to her?*
She sat in the car in Drew's driveway, trying to shake off Deanna's words of advice. Drew was standing at the door, waiting for her to get out of the car. He hugged her as hard as he could when she stepped into the house. She

smiled. She could tell that it had been a rough week for him. He hadn't shaved, and he looked tired.

She asked, "How was work?"

"It was fine."

"How have you been feeling?"

"I'm pretty good. Have you eaten?"

"Not since lunch."

"I just finished cooking. Would you like something to eat?"

"Sure."

Drew escorted Salida into the kitchen to eat. He bowed his head to pray as the two of them sat. She did the same. After praying, he stood to prepare a plate for Salida. Then, he sat it in front of her.

"Thanks."

"No problem."

He grabbed a smaller amount of food for himself. She watched as he sat his plate on the table.

"Are you on a diet or something?"

He shook his head, "No, I'm not that hungry."

"Okay." She began to eat. "This is really good!"

"Thanks."

Salida cleaned her plate in no time. Drew continued eating, taking small bites.

"Drew, can we talk?"

"Yeah."

"I really do want to be with you. I don't know any other way to show you this."

Drew listened as Salida went on about how things have been since he dropped her off that night.

"Salida, what do you want to do?"

"I want to be your wife? I'm so ready to make this work out for us."

He watched her as he asked, "Are you sure?"

"Yes, I'm sure." She rubbed her belly. "And we have our seed growing inside of me. How could I not be sure that I want to be with you?"

Drew smiled although he wasn't convinced. He decided to wait a while before returning the ring to Salida.

A week had gone by and Salida had been over every day. Drew enjoyed her company. He wanted to reassure her that he was willing to be the best husband and father he could be. He cooked for her, cleaned the kitchen, and watched her doze off every night. Then, he would head to the couch to watch whatever game was playing. He didn't care much for reality or talk shows, but he loved sports, especially basketball, football, and baseball.

Salida would roll over after Drew had left the room. She felt safe with Drew. If there was any man that could ever make her feel like a woman should feel, that would be Drew. She knew it. She knew that he would be everything that she needed him to be. She was also aware that he would do anything to keep her mind at ease. She stayed over every night that week to see if he would say anything about her coming over without calling. He never acknowledged it, never asked for time alone, and never changed his demeanor to make her feel that she was overcrowding him. Every night that week, Salida slept like a baby.

It was Saturday, and Drew decided that he would return the ring to its owner. He decided that he would do something really nice for the night.

Salida was working at the dealership that Saturday. There were a few employees that had called in, and she was badly needed. She was in the middle of a sale when the roses arrived. She blushed as her customers picked with her about her secret admirer.

After the sale, she called Drew.

"Hello?"

"Hey!"

"How are you?"

"I'm well, just received your roses."

"Really?"

"Yes, thank you! That really made my day."

Drew smiled on the other end. "Not a problem. So, how is your day going anyway?"

"It's fine. I get off around four. So, I'll be there after I go home, and take a shower."

"Okay."

"What are you doing?"

"I'm just touching up on a few things in the house."

"Oh, okay. Well, I have another customer that just pulled up. I'll call you back when I leave."

"Alright, I'll talk to you then."

It was cold outside, which was great for having a fireside dinner. There was a restaurant downtown in which one could eat outside around the fire pits while enjoying an array of music and some of the best food the town had to offer. It was a little pricey, but well worth it for the occasion. Drew went through his closet, searching for something nice to wear as his arms were larger from lifting weights at the gym.

Later, Salida called to inform Drew that she was leaving work, and would head over after taking a shower at her house.

Drew asked, "Can you wear something warm, but nice? I want to go out for dinner. You'll have to grab a coat too. It's really cold outside."

"Sure."

"Okay."

Salida arrived almost two hours later. She was well dressed for the occasion.

Drew was excited as he had never been out to this particular restaurant. "You look nice!"

Salida replied, "Thanks! You do too!"

"Thank you. Are you ready to leave?"

"Of course, I'm dang near starving."

"Really?"

"Yes."

"Do you want to grab something before we get there?"

"No, I can wait."

"Okay, let's go."

Salida was curious to know where Drew was taking her as he was very excited about heading out.

After arriving at the restaurant, and ordering their food, the two of them cuddled for a moment. "Now I know why you asked me to wear something warm."

"Yes, I'm glad you did. Are you still cold?"

"I'm not. The fire pits are keeping it really warm out here. There's a slight drift, but not enough for me to get cold." She looked around. "It's beautiful."

He smiled, "I'm glad you like it."

Salida realized that all Drew wanted was for her to be happy. He smiled about the small things that excited her, didn't want to do anything that made her feel uncomfortable, and acknowledged her whenever anyone was present. She loved that feeling.

Drew blessed the food after its arrival. After tasting it for the first time, he decided to share a piece with her. He grabbed another fork, and leaned it in her direction, "Taste!"

The aroma hit her nose as soon as he lifted it. "It smells really good." She removed the food from the fork, "That is good!"

"I know."

"My food is really good too. You should try it."

She slightly leaned back as he cut a piece for himself.

"Wow!"

"Good, huh?"

"Yes, extremely."

The two of them almost ate everything on their plate. They were both stuffed.

Drew lifted his eyebrow, "Would you like some dessert?"

"No, I'm full. I don't want to overeat."

"You're feeding two now."

"I know."

Curiously Drew asked, "Have you made an appointment yet?"

"I made one on Thursday. My appointment is Tuesday at two."

"I'll leave work early to go with you."

"Really, you want to go with me?"

"Of course I do! I'm clueless as to how this works. I was the youngest, remember."

"You have nieces and nephews."

"I know, but I wasn't there when they were born. I didn't go to any of the appointments either."

"Okay. I want you to go anyway. I'm a little nervous about it."

The two of them chatted away for another thirty minutes before they left. When they returned to the house, Salida was exhausted. Drew was wide awake, and rubbing his fingers through her curls as they watched television from his bed. Her presence alone gave him a feeling that he couldn't explain.

"Babe?"

"Yes," Salida replied.

He grabbed her hand, while reaching into his pocket. While sliding the ring back onto her finger, he said, "I'm returning this ring to you."

She smiled, and sat up to face him. She considered all that she had done. "I'm sorry about the way I made you feel before." She wrapped her arms around him. "I love you so much. I wasn't sure what I would have done without you."

Drew held her tight. He felt her weakening. Instead of taking pleasure in the moment, he advised her to get some rest. He tucked her in, and headed to the living room.

It was April 7th. The rain had been steady all morning. Drew and Salida decided to meet for lunch. Although they worked minutes from each other, the nicer restaurants were closer to the building in which he worked. She decided that she would pick him up. As he headed to her car, a SUV pulled ahead of her. Jonathan stepped out of the SUV, and opened the door. Jasmine ran past Drew, and jumped into the SUV with Jonathan. Drew got into the car with Salida.

"Hey!"

"That bitch!"

"What?"

"Jasmine just got into that SUV with Jonathan."

Confused by her anger, Drew said, "Okay. So, why does that matter to you?"

"That's my ex-husband! Friends don't do that!"

"Yeah, but you know how she is."

"It doesn't matter! That's not something you do!"

Drew sat silently, while Salida vented. She was fuming, and he sat listening to every profane word that came out of her mouth. She didn't stop until they pulled up to the restaurant.

"You know, I'm not even hungry anymore."

Drew looked in her direction, "Really?"

"Yes. I think that this has upset me to the point that I don't even feel like eating."

"Salida, our wedding is two months away. Are you sure that you're ready to do this?"

"What do you mean?"

"Things are going to happen that are beyond your control. Maybe, she has always liked him, and is finally getting a chance to see if things will work out for them. He's your ex for a reason, right?"

"This has nothing to do with our marriage! This has a lot to do with the line you don't cross with your friends!"

"But, why does it matter when you're with the person that you want to be with?"

"Because, that's my ex-husband!"

Salida began to get out of the car, but Drew never opened his door.

She turned towards the car, "Why aren't you getting out?"

"Take me back to work."

"What?"

"Take me back."

"Why?"

"Because, I have been sitting in this car the whole time, listening to you nag about seeing those two together. It shouldn't be a problem for you, but you are livid!"

She returned to the car, and closed the door. "Have you ever seen your ex with one of your close friends?"

"Yes! My best friend is married to someone I dated a long time ago. I don't hold that against him because I knew she wasn't for me. I was still the best man in the wedding. I was happy for both of them. From the moment they started dating, they were inseparable. That same glow still shows on their face when I see them."

"That sounds crazy to me!"

"Why? What if I would have stepped in, and told him that he can't be with my ex? I would have ruined what was destined to be. And, I do believe they were destined to be together. He's a really stocky guy that works out religiously. He's very hard core, but for her, he's soft. I've known him all my life, and never believed anyone could bring him to that point."

She thought about it for a while, considering the fact that Jonathan had walked out on her twice. She, then, agreed, "Well, I guess you're right... Let's get something to eat."

Their wedding day, June 29th, came quickly. Salida was six months pregnant and hardly showing. Although there were two others that were aware, Salida and Drew had both agreed to only tell their mothers about her pregnancy.

Both families were shocked to see the small bump as Salida walked down the aisle. As she walked, she checked the crowd in search of Jonathan. She knew that if anyone could possibly ruin her wedding, it would be Jonathan. She wasn't exactly sure how she would react to him showing up.

Everything about the wedding was beautiful. Tears rolled down everyone's face as Drew relay the vows he had written. The ceremony was short, but well planned.

Afterwards, everyone headed to the back of the building for the reception. The food choices were endless. Deanna and her boyfriend sat opposite Mr. and Mrs. Davison during the reception. She spent a vast majority of her time getting to know the couple. She smiled as she became familiar with the two, considering the conversation she had with Salida about how welcoming they were. Deanna sat back in her chair, pleased with Salida's new in-laws. She realized that even she would have a lot to learn from them.

Salida and Drew thanked everyone for coming out, and headed to the airport. At 6:15 p.m., the two of them were en route to Paris.

After the honeymoon, things were back to normal. Both Salida and Drew were working overtime, trying to have everything prepared for their baby's arrival. A month before the wedding, Salida rented out her home instead of selling it. The renters paid an additional three hundred dollars every month, which would assist Salida in paying off her car. Drew's car was already paid off. Any extra income was deposited into a joint savings the two of them had opened. They both realized how much they were able to save by working together. Drew paid the mortgage, insurance, and electric bill. Salida handled all of the other expenses. They also agreed on a stick-to-it grocery budget.

Although Salida complained that it was decreasing their savings, Drew paid his tithes faithfully. He tried to explain the blessing in tithing. He wanted her to be able to understand the covering over their life when they gave, but she couldn't. He read every portion of the Bible that pertained to tithing, but it only frustrated her even more. She argued, "We're not paying God, we're decreasing the amount of money that we're able to save for our daughter! God doesn't need money!"

Drew became exhausted with the argument. He continued tithing, using the money that he deposited into his personal account. Afterwards, He realized that this was no longer a discussion between the two of them.

Drew did all that he could to child-proof his home. He knew the baby wouldn't be able to crawl or walk for a while, but he wanted to be prepared for it all. He also attended classes with Salida to know what to expect when she goes into labor, things that are needed when she heads to the hospital, and small things that he must do to make life easier for mom. Some of the classes scared Drew to death. He watched as other couples argued over the smallest things. There was a couple that argued from the moment they walked into the door. Another couple that attended the meetings argued quietly. The wife always seemed annoyed by every touch she received from her husband, as if she were disgusted with his existence. The husband seemed to not even know where to touch her to keep her from feeling that way. Drew sat, watching the couples, wondering what anyone could have done to bring them to that point. *How can people walk around arguing all of the time? Why wouldn't a woman want to be touched by her own husband?* He considered the longevity of the other relationships. Then, he considered his own. Other than the issue of tithing, Salida seemed very

91

happy with him. At night, she moved her body as close to him as she possibly could, as if it was her way of reassuring herself that he was there. They also continued taking walks through the park. They would have lunch together, but it wasn't as frequent as it was before they were married. Drew was okay with it because he didn't like to feel overcrowded, or as if he were overcrowding her. Although they were married, he still enjoyed his personal time. He would leave the house to visit his friends with no complaints from Salida. He loved the feeling. He smiled, knowing that things were different for them.

On October 1st, around 6 a.m., Salida went into labor. During her last appointment, she was advised that she was dilating, and the baby could come at any moment. Therefore, their bags were already packed, and sitting in the car. Drew fearfully assisted Salida to the car. Although she was in pain, she couldn't help but laugh at the fact that Drew was sweating as if it were the hottest day of the year.

Drew struggled to get himself together as they headed to the hospital only blocks away from their home. He called his and Salida's mother to let them know that they were headed to the hospital. Both families had already packed their bags, and were headed in the direction of the hospital to see their new grandchild after receiving the call from Drew. Drew's parents also brought along a basket, given to Drew's mother from the church, of clothing, diapers, and small necessities the baby would need during its first year. There were enough clothes for twins.

Deanna was the first one to arrive. She sat in the waiting room, not wanting to witness Salida's labor pains. After seeing Drew for a short period of time, she knew that going in the delivery room wouldn't be a great idea.

At 11:24 a.m. October 1st, Drew welcomed his daughter, Alana Monet Davison. Tears of joy flowed from his face as he held his baby for the first time. He kissed her forehead, and handed her to Salida for feeding. As the nurses began to leave, he stepped out of the room to gather his thoughts. He also headed towards the waiting room to get Salida's mother. He could smell the smoke on her clothing as he approached her.

"Has she had the baby?"

"Yes ma'am!"

Deanna lit up like the Fourth of July. "Can I see her?"

"Sure."

They headed towards the room. So bad he wanted to advise her to Lysol herself down, or go back to the waiting room, not wanting his newborn to have to breathe in those fumes. Instead he walked ahead of her, not wanting her to see the look of annoyance on his face.

He opened the door for her as they entered the room. Salida grinned from ear to ear to see that her mother was present. Drew felt some relief when Deanna walked to the opposite side of the room, took off her jacket, and washed her hands before holding Alana.

Deanna held her hands out for Alana. She was able to get a better view of her whenever Salida removed the cloth that covered a portion of her face. Deanna exclaimed "Awe, she's beautiful! Look at her!"

Drew and Salida smiled. Drew grabbed the camera to take a picture of Deanna holding Alana.

Drew's parents arrived at 12:45. His father was a little exhausted from the drive, but was very excited to get a glimpse of Alana. Drew's mother cried when realizing that her baby finally had a child of his own.

At 1:15, Drew decided to leave to grab a bite to eat along with his parents and Deanna, while Salida and Alana rested. After eating, he advised everyone to go and rest at his house. His parents had already purchased a room at the hotel, and decided to check in and rest for a few hours. Deanna headed over to Drew's to sleep in the guestroom. Drew headed back to the hospital. He didn't want to leave Salida and Alana alone for too long. As he headed back to the hospital, he called Tamara.

"Hello?"

"What are you doing?"

"Working, what are you doing?"

"Headed back to the hospital."

"She had the baby?"

"Yes, her name is Alana Monet."

Tamara smiled, "Congrats, Drew!"

"Thanks!"

"Man! You're a father now!"

"I know! It's cool, huh?"

"Of course it's cool! I didn't think you would ever have any kids!"

"Whatever."

Tamara laughed. "I'm playing, but I am happy for you. So, when will I get a chance to see Alana?"

"I just pulled up to the hospital. I'll send you a picture as soon as I park my car."

"Have Mr. and Mrs. D seen her?"

"They're here."

"Wow! That is great."

"Yeah, they made it in around one or so."

"Oh, okay."

"I'm about to send you the picture."

"Okay. Well, I have to go now. I'm going to call you whenever I leave."

"Okay," replied Drew. He hung up the phone, sent the picture, and headed back into the hospital.

Drew kissed Salida's forehead after walking into the room. She smiled, but her eyes were still closed.

"How do you feel?"

"I feel drained. I was awake for a while after you left. I didn't want to drift into a deep sleep while you were gone, especially with Alana here."

"Why didn't you say something before I left? I would have stayed here, and let our parents grab something to eat alone."

"It's okay."

"Well, I'm here. I'm not going anywhere. So, you can rest."

"Aren't you tired?"

"A little, but I can grab some coffee or something."

"Are you sure?"

"Yes. If I get too sleepy, I'll let you know."

"Okay."

Salida turned over to get comfortable. Drew sat in a chair between Salida and Alana, reading magazines that he had grabbed downstairs. He was exhausted, but was reassured before-hand that there would be days like this, days where he needed to stay awake so that Salida could rest. He considered the fact that she had just been through hours of labor, and needed it. Therefore, he sat in the chair, waiting for his turn to do the same.

For years, things worked out well for the two of them. They had written a schedule that allowed both of them to be able to drop Alana off and pick her up from daycare. Drew would come home and cook, while Salida fed Alana. They were even able to take walks in the park, and have time to themselves when needed. Life was grand. Alana seemed to have been growing and growing daily. Drew and Salida enjoyed every moment, from crawling and walking to saying "Da Da" for the first time.

It wasn't until months before Alana's fifth birthday that all of this changed for them. Salida was sitting at her desk, finishing the paperwork from a sale, when Chelsea knocked at her door.

"Hey! Come in."

Chelsea entered the office. "I didn't want anything. There's some guy here asking for you. I wasn't sure if you wanted anyone to let him know that you were here or not. So, I told him to give me a minute to see if you're here."

"What does he look like?"

"He's super hot! He's tall, muscular, and extremely handsome."

"What's his name?"

"It's something with a "J", like John or Joe. I don't remember."

"You can let him know that I'm here."

"Okay." Chelsea curiously walked away. She had never seen this guy at the dealership, and knew he wasn't there to buy a car after seeing the vehicle he was already driving. She checked her own appearance through the glass as she headed in his direction. "Sir, Mrs. Davison is here. You can follow me to her office."

Jon followed her, noticing that her twist had become extreme. He laughed to himself as he continued walking towards Salida's office. Chelsea stepped into the office and asked if Salida would like for her to close the door.

"Yes, please."

"Okay," Chelsea replied as she closed the door, and headed to her office.

Jon continued standing in the doorway, staring at Salida.

"Would you like to sit?"

"Not really."

"Okay. So, how can I help you?"

Jon rolled his eyes. "You can't just sit there, acting like I'm some stranger that needs to purchase a car."

Salida replied, "I know who you are. However, I don't know why you're here."

"I came to take back what belongs to me. Do you know how hard these last few years have been for me, knowing that you and some guy have a child together? You all are walking around like a big, happy family."

"We are happy! If you don't remember, you walked out on me, looking at me as if you were disgusted! Plus, the last time I saw you, you were holding the door for Jasmine as she was getting in your car. You seemed to be happy also."

"Jasmine's a slut! She's always been jealous of you. When I realized she was only trying to stir up something, I totally walked away from her. She's been in your relationship since you and that guy had started dating. She even called me to tell me that you were dating him. That time I showed up at the restaurant, and you were there with him, she had called me then."

Salida was astounded. She knew that Jonathan wasn't lying. "Why? Why would she do something like that?"

"She's always tried to cause confusion in your relationships. She's just messy. She came to my house, wanting to sleep with me. She figured that since you were getting married, I was all hers. When I rejected her, she asked if we had still been sleeping together. She told me that she could make me forget about you."

"Wow!" Salida didn't want to believe Jon, but she knew how conniving Jasmine could be. She knew that Jasmine would go to any extent to get what she wanted. She sat in her chair, considering everything. Jonathan continued talking, but Salida stopped him, "You know... it doesn't even matter now. I'm a married woman, and I really do love Drew."

Jonathan slammed his hand on her desk, "Don't talk like that! It angers me to no end that you went ahead and married him. How could you do that to us? How could you go on, acting like we didn't have a family before? We could have had another child, and raised him like we did Chris. Chris was a good boy. He was our little angel."

Salida began to break, "Please stop. Please don't talk about him."

"He was our son. How do you think he would feel, knowing that you have moved on and created another family with someone else? How do you think he would feel with you acting like his little sister is better?"

"If Chris was here, I would never do that. Chris is not here, Jon. He's not coming back."

"Lida, do you know how I feel knowing that my son will never walk through that door again? Can you imagine what it feels like to lose my wife and my child?"

"You lost your wife by choice."

"Lida, you didn't even try. You didn't even attempt to call me when I walked out."

"I wasn't supposed to, Jon! If you loved me as much as you said you did, you wouldn't have walked out. You would have stayed to help me raise Alana whether she was yours or not."

Jon held his head down. "You're right... You're right." He turned to leave. "I'm going to let you get back to work." He turned the knob on the door. "I haven't changed my number. When you realize that it's not too late for us, call me. I realize something. When you truly love someone, no matter what you've done to cover it, it doesn't die. I've made mistakes, and let you down, but if you still love me, you'll be back. It always happens that way. I love you, Lida. So, I'll be waiting." Jon walked out. Salida went back to work, trying to pretend that this had never happened.

Moments later, Chelsea knocked at the door. "Salida?"

"Come on in."

"Are you okay?"

"Yeah, I'm fine. Why'd you ask me that?"

"I was walking by when I heard that guy tell you that he loved you before he opened the door."

"It doesn't matter."

"Does he know that you're married?"

"He does."

"I know that I'm being nosey..."

"You are being nosey. You always are."

Chelsea was offended. She knew Salida was right. "Sorry." She headed towards the door.

"Chelsea, will you sit down for a minute?"

"Sure."

"You're nosey, but you're also one of my closest friends. I know that even when you're digging for information, you never share what I tell you with anyone. That's what I like about you."

Chelsea smiled as Salida continued. "However, I realize that you only do this because your relationship is crazy. You want reassurance that your relationship isn't as bad as it seems."

"How do you know that?"

"It shows all over your face."

"Is it that obvious?"

"For me it is. Please don't be that way. We've been friends since I started working here. I'm not competing with you. I truly want the best for you."

"I know you do. Things just aren't working out for me."

"Give it time. Things will change. If your boyfriend knows what I know about you, he would never let you go."

"Thanks!"

"That guy that left was my ex-husband. We have a lot of history together. We even dated in high school."

"Wow! He's very attractive. What caused you two to separate?"

Salida sighed, "Before you knew me, I had a son." She took a picture of Christopher out of her drawer.

Chelsea held the photo, "He's so cute!"

"He was very cute." Salida took a deep breath as she began to explain things to Chelsea, "We were at the grocery store one day. His teacher had called earlier that day to tell me what a great kid he was, and how well he was doing in kindergarten. I wanted to give him a treat. So, I told him to run to the car to get an extra quarter to use the gumball machine." Salida smiled. "He loved the huge gumballs! There were some men driving around in the parking lot as I stood at the front of the store, watching and waiting for Chris to return. As he headed back to me, one of the guys started shooting at the store."

"Why?"

"I don't know."

Chelsea covered her mouth in shock, "Oh my!" She had already figured out what happened before Salida told her.

Salida wiped the tears from her eyes, "Right before I had him in my arms, the guy shot him. Chris took his last breathe, while falling into my arms."

Tears began to run down Chelsea's face, "How could someone be so careless?"

Salida shook her head, "I don't know. Can you imagine what it feels like to lose someone that way?" She held her hand against her chest. "He was right there. My son died instantly with his head on my chest."

Chelsea couldn't take anymore. She couldn't control the tears that fell. She grabbed Kleenex after Kleenex, wiping away the tears, "I'm so sorry, Salida. I'm so sorry."

"No need to apologize." Salida said as she wiped away her own tears. "That guy that left was my son's father. Our relationship went downhill after Chris' death. I don't think he's ever forgiven me for it."

"It wasn't your fault!"

"He knows that. Everyone told him what happened. There was no way that we could bring our son back." Salida smiled. "Chris was so precious, so innocent. He was Jon's pride and joy. No one ever expects for their child's life to be cut short so unexpectedly. It doesn't seem fair."

"How old was he when he died?"

"He was five. That was the last picture he had taken before he was killed."

"Wow, how do you feel now?"

"I'm okay. It still hurts. It bothers me a little more now."

"Why?"

"Alana will be five this year. It scares me."

"She'll be fine. Nothing's going to happen to Alana."

"I pray that it doesn't. Sometimes, I feel as if I shouldn't even be there, as if she's safer if I'm not present."

"You shouldn't talk like that."

"I know. Being a parent is a challenge. We do everything to protect our kids, trying to lead them down the right path, letting them know that we love them and care about their well-being. It's hard to not feel as if I will let Alana down after witnessing what happened to Chris. Every day, for a long time, I wondered if things would have been different had I have gone to the car myself, or gone with him. He was so happy to go to the car by himself. He felt like a little man, always wanting to do things on his own. He has truly been missed."

Chelsea shook her head. She couldn't fathom having something like that to happen to her. Her heart hurt deeply for Salida.

"How have you been able to cope with it?"

"For a long time, I couldn't. At some point in time, I tried to walk away from everything that made me think of him. I quit my job, rented out my home, and stored all of my memories of Chris in a box that I buried in the back yard, including the quarter that he held in his hand when he was shot. I even stayed away from my family."

"Did it help?"

"No, it made me hurt even more."

"So, what did you do?"

"I moved back into my home, dug up the box, and started working here."

"How did that make you feel?"

"I felt better; being able to think of the good times that I had with him helped out a lot."

Chelsea took a deep breath, "I have to get back to my office. I have a few more sales to finish."

"No problem."

"Thank you so much for sharing your story. I truly appreciate it."

"Thank you for listening!"

"Whenever you feel like chatting. Just call me. Have you ever told Drew about this?"

"I haven't."

"Why?"

"Because I didn't ever want him to feel that Jon was a threat to our relationship. If he knew that I had a son before Alana, he would probably keep her away from me after finding out what happened."

"You shouldn't feel that way. I believe that Drew is a very understanding man. With everything that you have told me about him, I think this would bring you guys even closer."

"Maybe, but I don't want to take any chances. I love Drew. He's been very good to me and Alana."

Chelsea headed out of the office. As she made it to the door, she said, "I know I am not the smartest person, or the person you would rely on for answers in regards to your marriage, but if you are going to spend the rest of your life with Drew, you really need to let him know about your son. I can't understand why you would keep this from him."

Salida didn't respond. Instead, she sat with her head down as if she were too engulfed in her work to acknowledge that Chelsea was still standing in the doorway.

After Chelsea left, everything that Jonathan said played in Salida's head over and over again. Even after having a child with him, she never loved Drew as much. Jonathan had her heart, and he knew it. He knew everything about her. Because of this, he knew that he'd always have an advantage over anyone, and could always talk his way back into her life.

After work, Salida headed home. She contemplated calling Jonathan several times before she made it there. She was glad that she didn't, but she knew that every day would be a challenge for her until she did. Salida sat in the driveway, thinking of what her mother had said about her marrying someone else's husband. She closed her eyes and placed her hands over her face, not believing that after being married for almost five years, she was still in love with another man. Eventually, she got out of the car, walked into the house, and greeted her family as she does every day. Drew had just finished preparing dinner.

"Good evening," she said.

"Good evening! How was work?"

"It was fine."

Alana ran into the room, wrapping her arms around her mother's leg as she always does, "Mommy!"

"Hey, Baby!" Salida picked up Alana. "How was daycare?"

"Fun!"

"Oh yeah? What did you do?"

"We learned a new word, and we played in the centers."

"What was your word for today?"

"Persistent. I used it in a sentence when I was talking to my friend."

"Really? What did you say?"

"She was getting mad because she couldn't tie her shoe. I bent down to tie them for her, but told her that she has to be persistent."

"You're such a smart girl!"

Alana smiled. Salida put Alana down, and headed towards the room. As she began to undress, Drew walked into the room. "What's wrong?"

Salida turned to him, "What are you talking about?"

"You didn't kiss me when you walked in. That's unusual."

"I had onions on my sandwich today. I didn't want you to taste them."

He folded his arms as he watched her. She sighed, "Are you finished cooking all of the food?"

"Yes, but it has to cool down a little before we eat."

"Can you give me a minute to change clothes?"

"Sure."

"Without you standing there watching me?"

"Huh?" Salida's comment confused Drew.

"You're just standing there, watching me as if I'm some car on display!"

"Are you serious?"

Salida turned to Drew. Angrily, she said, "Can you get out for a minute?"

"What if I want to be in here with you?"

Frustrated with Drew, Salida said, "Right now, I want to be in here by myself. Can you give me a moment to just think?"

Drew was dumbfounded. He'd never been put out of his own room. He'd watched her undress on numerous occasions, and she had never said anything. Not wanting to argue, he walked away.

Salida locked the door as soon as Drew walked out. She put on something comfortable and lay across the bed, thinking of what Jon was probably doing at that very moment, wondering how he had been coping without her for so many years. She thought of how good he smelled when he walked in her office earlier, how the scent lingered after he had left. She also noticed that he was thinner, but even more attractive. Ten minutes later, she fell asleep.

Drew sat in the living room, waiting for Salida to come out of the room. Alana ran into the room, "I'm hungry, Daddy!"

"Okay. Do you want to wait on Mommy or do you want to go ahead and eat?"

"What is Mommy doing?"

"I'm not sure."

"Can I go and ask her?"

Drew smiled. "No, I think Mommy is a little tired, or something."

"Okay. Well, I would like to eat." Alana folded her arms. Drew laughed to himself as he stood to prepare a plate for Alana. After preparing her meal, he prayed and headed back to the living room.

Alana called to him, "Daddy?"

"Yes."

"Can you stay in here while I eat?"

"Sure."

Drew grabbed a magazine, and began to read as Alana ate.

"The food is really good, Daddy!"

"Thank you?"

"I love the chicken! It tastes just right!"

Drew laughed. He didn't bother letting her know that she wasn't eating chicken. Instead, he continued reading the magazine.

"Daddy, are you going to eat?"

"I'm waiting on your mom."

Alana shook her head, "I don't think she's that hungry. She's been in the room for a long time."

Drew agreed, "I know. I think she is sleeping." He checked his watch. Thirty minutes had gone by since she had put him out of the room. The food was getting cold, and Drew was hungry. He grabbed a plate, and began to eat with Alana.

Eating with her father excited Alana, "Thanks for eating with me!"

"No problem. I was trying to wait on your mom, but I was hungry."

Alana wanted to say something to reassure Drew that eating without Salida was okay. She shrugged, "Maybe she ate before she came home. Now, she doesn't want anything to eat."

Drew chuckled, "You're so grown!"

"That's what my teacher says all of the time."

"Does she? Why does she say that?"

She tilted her head as if she were trying to think of a reason. Then, she shrugged, "I don't know."

Drew washed the dishes after he and Alana finished eating. Afterwards, he lied down on the sofa to watch television. Alana lied on his chest, watching the show with him. Eventually, the two of them fell asleep.

Salida unlocked the bedroom door around eight. She walked into the living room to find Alana sleeping on top of Drew. She awakened Drew by pulling Alana off of him. He went to the room to shower, while Salida began to prepare Alana for bed.

After taking a shower, Drew jumped in the bed. He was exhausted from assisting other workers on top of completing his own work. Having to deal with Salida's episode, after picking up Alana and coming home to cook, didn't make things any better. He hadn't lied down for five minutes before he was asleep.

Over a period of time, Salida's episodes seemed to increase. Drew wasn't sure what was going on with her. Every time he tried to console or talk to her, she seemed annoyed, never giving him the opportunity to resolve the issue with her. She also began to come home from work later than normal. One day, as she came home from work, Drew stood in the doorway of the kitchen.

"Good evening," She said while rolling her eyes as if his presence alone bothered her.

"Salida, we need to talk."

"I'm tired, and I don't feel like talking."

"You haven't felt like talking for a while now, but you have to tell me what's going on."

Salida headed towards the room. Drew followed.

"Drew, can I have some privacy?"

"Privacy doesn't exist when we live in the same house."

She turned to him, "Are you serious?"

"Yes, I am!" Drew shook his head, "You've been acting so different lately. Everything that we've done on a normal basis since we have been married has started to bother you now. I've also noticed that you've been spending more money, but I never see what you spend it on." Drew held up his cell phone. "Technology allows me to get a text every time you swipe the card. You've been swiping the hell out of the card, even when you tell me that you're working over. What's going on with you?"

"Why does it even matter to you?"

"Why wouldn't it matter to me?" Drew continued, "You're not here when you're supposed to be. If you want to hang out with your friends, at least, let me know where you are. You've been coming home late....." Drew thought of everything that he was saying. He didn't want to accuse her of cheating. Instead, he said, "If you don't want to be here, let me know."

"Drew, I'm here! We have a daughter that will be five in two weeks."

"Is she the only reason why you're here?"

"No, she's not."

"Right now, our marriage reminds me of the couple that was coming to the classes when you were pregnant. The wife didn't want to be touched by her husband. She always seemed annoyed with him. I don't want to be in a marriage like that. If you feel that you want to be elsewhere, be there. I will not allow myself to stay in a marriage like that."

Salida held her head down. "Drew, it's not you. It's me. I haven't been happy with myself."

"What makes you unhappy?"

"I think I'm just drained by my job. So, I go shopping after work to just relieve my stress."

"I've never known you to shop like this. You've been spending a lot of money."

"I know. I'm sorry."

"Do you want to take a vacation or something after Alana's birthday?"

"Yes, we can."

"Where do you want to go?"

"I'm not sure... Not too far."

"I'll call my mom, and ask her to watch Alana while we go out of town."

"Okay."

"Is there anything else that you want to talk about?"

Salida shook her head. "No."

"Why haven't you told me this before?"

"Because I know that your job is stressful too. You haven't been able to move up like you want. Your manager is full of himself. I'm sure that by now your manager knows how intelligent you are. He also knows that you have the ability to handle your job without his supervision, but he still has a tendency to micro-manage everyone."

"That's true, but it's not always about me. I don't want our jobs to affect our marriage."

"You're right."

"Let's do something tonight."

"Like what?"

"We can go out to eat, take Alana to the movies," Drew threw his hands up, "Or whatever you want to do."

Salida smiled, "Let's go out to eat. You'll have to be the designated driver because I want a drink."

Drew laughed, "Okay, We can do that."

Even after agreeing to do better, Salida still continued to come home late. Her episodes weren't as often, but she had them. After Alana's birthday, they seemed to increase again. She also forfeited the trip they were supposed to take. Drew was flabbergasted. He tried to do whatever he could to get things under control. Every attempt to discuss the issue failed. He even tried to get a counselor for the two of them, but she assured him that she wouldn't come. The fact that he considered a counselor, seemed to upset her even more. Therefore, she began to sleep in the room with Alana. The harder he tried to keep them together, the more she began to pull away. Drew felt as if he were in a no-win situation.

Thanksgiving was coming quickly. Drew thought that going to Salida's hometown, and being around her family would put her at ease a little more. He called Deanna to see if everyone would be home for Thanksgiving.

"Hello?"

"How are you?"

"I'm fine. Who is this?"

"It's Andrew, Salida's husband."

"Oh, how are you?"

"I'm doing well. I was just calling to see if you all were having Thanksgiving dinner at your place. Salida has been under a lot of stress here lately. I thought that being around her family would put her at ease."

"Yes, we're having Thanksgiving dinner. It would be great to have you all here...." Deanna added, "I talked to Salida just the other day. She did seem a little different, almost as if she was agitated."

Drew agreed, "Yes ma'am, that's how she'd been acting. I've tried to make things better for her, but nothing that I do is working."

"Don't worry. We'll get her back in shape. I have just the right thing for her."

Drew hesitated. Deanna's words worried him. "Okay. Well, we'll see you then."

"Alright...how's my grandbaby?"

"She's great, just growing up on us."

"I know she is... well, I'll chat with you later. Call me if you need me."

"Okay."

Drew hung up. As much as he hated the smell of smoke, he was sure that Deanna had something up her sleeves to get Salida in order. He felt better already.

Drew, Salida, and Alana arrived at Deanna's the day before Thanksgiving. He was so glad to see Deanna standing in the doorway when they arrived. Salida was also glad to see her mom. She awakened Alana. "Come on! We're here!"

They all jumped out of the car, and rushed to greet Deanna. Alana yelled, "Granny!"

Deanna hugged Alana as hard as she could, "How's my grandbaby doing?"

"I'm fine."

"You're just growing up!"

"I know. I'm getting taller too!"

Deanna laughed, "Yes, you are!"

Alana ran into the house to see if her other cousins had made it in. Salida, then, hugged her mother. "Hey!"

"How are you?"

"I'm well!"

Deanna looked at her for a minute. Drew was standing behind Salida. Deanna reached for him, "How's my son-in law?"

"I'm well," Drew said as he hugged her back. He noticed that he didn't smell cigarette smoke as her hugged her. "You stopped smoking!"

Deanna smiled, "I did! How'd you know?"

"I didn't smell it when you hugged me! That's great!"

"Yes! I've been going to the gym too! After I stopped smoking, I started gaining a little weight. Since I've been in that gym, I feel so much better, and I have the men watching me!"

Drew laughed, "You're something else!"

Deanna chuckled, "I know!"

Salida interrupted, annoyed that Drew and Deanna were getting along so well, "I'm going to go in and check out the rest of the family."

Deanna checked Drew's expression. Drew threw his hands up. They began to follow Salida. Noticing that they were behind her, she turned to reassure them, "You two could have continued your conversation. You didn't have to follow me in here."

Deanna objected, "Oh, be quiet! Why are you acting so crazy?"

"I'm just saying. You two were acting like old buddies."

"You should be glad. Some men don't even get along with their in-laws." She tapped Salida's shoulder, "You didn't even notice that I stopped smoking, but Drew did."

Salida rolled her eyes, "That's only because your smoke was making him sick. Now, he doesn't have to deal with it."

"Well, that's a good thing!"

"Maybe."

Deanna couldn't believe Salida's response. She was certain that their marriage was in trouble. She looked back at Drew, "Go ahead and get your bags out of the car. You all can sleep in the same room you always sleep in. I washed the sheets last night because I knew you all were coming."

Drew replied, "Yes ma'am." He headed towards the door. So bad, he wanted to jump in the car, and head back to his house. Instead, he opened the trunk to get their bags.

While Drew was getting the bags from the car, Deanna pulled Salida into her room. "What is your problem?"

Salida replied, "What are you talking about?"

"You know what I'm talking about. Why are you treating him that way?"

"How am I treating him?"

"Like you can't stand to be around him! What has he done to deserve that kind of treatment?"

"I'm not mistreating him!"

"Yes, you are!" Deanna folded her arms, "And you're cheating!"

"No, I'm not!"

Deanna nodded her head, "You are... Remember when I told you that you were marrying someone else's husband? That's because I knew then that it wasn't going to work between the two of you. You were still in love with Jon."

"How would you know that? Why are you in my relationship anyway? You're not married."

"Yeah, but I've been married before. I know what it's like to be on the other end. He came home late, spending all of the money by taking the other woman out, and snapping on me for no reason. Karma is a bitch, and you better be careful! Remember the saying: When the going gets tough, the tough gets going? Jon walked out on you during the toughest time of your life, even blaming you for what happened. Even after putting up with your smart mouth and negative comments, Drew is still there. You better get it together before you lose what's good for you. There's something about him that caused you to marry him. You better find that thing, and hang on to it. Otherwise, you're going to lose him."

"How do you know that it's Jon?"

"It's always been Jon. You've been after him forever, no matter how he's made you feel."

Salida turned her back, "I'm not sleeping with him."

"Not now, but it's just a matter of time. You should read what the Bible has to say about it. Don't send yourself to hell. He comes around when it's convenient to him. If he loved you, you would have never had the chance to get to know someone else enough to marry them. He would have been there."

"Okay, let's not talk about this anymore! I get it!"

Deanna folded her arms with uncertainty, "Okay."

Drew finished packing the bags, and sat down on the bed. He was tired, but didn't know if it was from the drive, or from Salida. He thrust his body over the bed, wanting to take a nap. Moments later, Salida walked into the room. "I see you finished packing."

Drew nodded, "Yes, I did."

"Are you tired?"

"For some reason I feel like I have no energy. I'm going to lie down for a while."

Salida noticed that Drew could barely keep his eyes open. "Okay. I'm going to go up front and check on Alana. I'll be back in here later on."

In no time, Drew had fallen asleep.

The rest of the trip wasn't so bad. Drew awakened early the next morning and helped Deanna prepare some of the Thanksgiving dinner. He also cooked breakfast for everyone, using the food that Deanna had purchased. Once again, breakfast was a hit. Everyone thanked him for breakfast.

Salida was also nice during the rest of the trip. Drew was excited to see her acting like his wife again. He didn't say anything to let her know that he noticed the difference in her. Instead, he sat, enjoying the moment, hoping that she didn't change once they were back home.

Alana also enjoyed the trip. She was able to spend time with all of her cousins as they played different games inside and outside. She also slept in the room with her grandmother. This was Deanna's decision because she didn't get to see her as often as she saw her other grandchildren. This was also how Deanna found out that Salida wasn't sleeping with Drew.

After everyone had finished eating dinner, Deanna insisted that the women clean the kitchen. After calling to check on his family, Drew sat and watched the game with the men. He didn't care much for beer, but a football game was always great to watch, especially when two of his favorite teams were playing.

Deanna and Salida washed dishes while everyone else fixed plates to take home, and wrapped up the leftovers. While everyone was distracted, Deanna asked Salida, "How long have you been sleeping in Alana's room?" Salida snapped, "How do you know that? That's none of your business." "Kids tell everything. Alana told me when she slept in my room. Don't you spank her for telling me either. We were just talking."

Salida continued washing dishes, trying to ignore Deanna. Deanna continued, "Why are you doing this to him?" She felt so sorry for Drew. Salida replied, "Why do you care? You didn't even like him at first, talking about his uppity family, asking what was wrong with him. What is it? Is it because he buys for you every Christmas and Mother's day?"

"That has nothing to do with it. The day I met his family, I gained much respect for them. I learned a lot from them, and kept in contact with his mother. They are one of the sweetest families I know. Talking to them motivated me to stop smoking, and get myself together. I've never felt this good. Yes, at first, I thought they would be a group that looked down on us. They embraced us, making us feel no different from anyone else. We don't have as much money as they do, but they don't care. They're a great family to be around. Had you not married Andrew, I would have never seen the difference."

Salida saw the sincerity in Deanna's face. She knew that she was right. Drew had an amazing family. Anyone that could get Deanna to stop smoking had to be amazing.

For the first time ever, Drew dreaded leaving Deanna's. He was certain that the demon that had entered Salida's body would return as soon as they entered the car. He prayed before they left, asking God to send that demon far away from his home. He was glad to have his wife back, and wanted things to stay that way.
Deanna hugged Alana, "Promise that you will be a good girl for your mom and dad."
Alana agreed, "I promise!"
Deanna smiled, "Okay, I know you will. Keep up the good work!"
Alana ran to the car. Salida was next. Deanna embraced her, "Take heed to everything that we talked about."
Salida rolled her eyes, not wanting to revisit the conversation. "I will."
Then, Deanna hugged Drew, "Thank you for helping me with the food! It's always a pleasure to have you here!"
Drew smiled, "Thank you for allowing me to assist you in the kitchen, and letting us stay here!"
"Not a problem. I'll see you all later."
The family hurried out to the car, and headed home, not wanting to lose any sleep for work the next day.

Things were better when they returned. Salida began to sleep in the room again. This transition didn't go over well for Alana. She had gotten used to sleeping with her mother. However, she knew that Salida would eventually return to her own room.
Drew was excited about the return. He was glad to see that his wife was slowly getting it together. The more that she returned to the norm, the more he desired to do things to keep her that way. He knew that Salida liked to try a different restaurant every month. He considered using this to his advantage. Therefore, he began to make different foods in the kitchen. He whipped up sauces, using different spices. During his lunch, he went online to view different foods he could make, while adding his own flavor. He purchased fresh foods from the market, giving his meals an extremely desirable taste.
Salida loved it. Drew's creativity caused her to invite friends and coworkers over for dinner. Her desire to try a different restaurant decreased with

every meal. Although she would never admit it, she couldn't wait to get home from work every day to see what Drew had cooked.

For months, things were much better than before. However, Salida continued to spend time with Jonathan. One day, as they were enjoying lunch, he expressed his impatience with her marriage. He grabbed her hands with his own, "Don't you think it's time to let this guy know that you don't want to be there?"

"Jon, I don't want to talk about this."

"We've been spending our days together for almost a year now. It's annoying when different holidays come around and you're not there."

"You know that I can't be with you like that. It's not like I'm breaking up with someone to be with you. I'm married to Drew."

"Do you enjoy your time with me?"

"I do."

"Then, why wouldn't you want to be there, lying beside me at night, taking trips with me to different countries, enjoying every season together like we used to?"

"Jon, you know that I would love to do that. My daughter is going to start Kindergarten this year. I can't just walk away from my family like that."

"We can start over, Lida. I really want this to happen for us. We'll fly all over the world, enjoying every moment together. I was looking online last night, and saw some reasonable flights to Italy. I would love for you to come with me."

Salida was excited, "You know that I've always wanted to go there! Jon, why are you doing this to me?"

He brushed her loose strands behind her ear with his fingers, "Lida, my patience is leaving me. You have to make up your mind. If you're going to be with me, be with me. I've been trying to win you back for a while now. You're running out of time."

Salida dropped her head.

He added, "I've also met someone else. So, this is my last draw. I can't keep sleeping alone like this."

Jonathan stood, paid for the food, and walked away. Salida returned to work.

After work, Salida drove to the park, needing time to think. Since lunch, she had been a mental mess. She cringed when thinking about Jonathan spending time with another woman. She knew that it wouldn't be hard for him to find someone else, but the thought of him actually loving another woman gave Salida heartburn.

She considered Drew's response to her walking out on him. She knew that he would try even harder to make things work if she admitted that she wanted to leave. She also knew that taking Alana wasn't an option as Drew would fight her to the very end. Therefore, she decided to slowly pull away, buying and saving things that she knew she would need to get another place. Knowing that she would have to walk away from Alana made her sick. However, Salida felt that Alana would be better without her.

On June 29th, Drew and Alana walked into the house after he picked her up from daycare. Everything seemed normal. Drew walked into his room, and noticed a note on his bed. He sat on his bed, unable to believe what he was reading. His heart beat faster as his body began to break down. He closed his eyes. Tears began to fall. He crumbled the paper, and tossed it across the room. He was broken. *How could she do this to us? What did I do wrong? What about our daughter?* Those were the only questions that he could think to ask himself. He stood to check the closet. All of her clothes and shoes were gone. Every piece of jewelry that he had ever purchased for her was missing, except her wedding ring. Her ring had been placed in the jewelry box. Drew's heart dropped as he picked up the ring he had purchased for the woman in which he had planned to spend the rest of his life. He cut off the light, closed the bathroom door, slid to the floor, and wept.

"Daddy?" Alana stood in the doorway of the room.

Drew, while clearing his throat, replied, "Yes, Babe?"

"What are we eating?"

"I'm not sure. Are you hungry?"

"Yes sir."

"Okay, give me just a minute. I'll be out, and we can go grab a bite to eat."

"Is mommy going to be late tonight?"

Holding back the hurt, Drew replied, "I'm not sure. I'll give her a call in a minute. Why don't you go in your room and play until I finish using the restroom?"

"Okay." Alana raced back to her room to play with her dolls. Drew tried to stand, but all of his energy had been taken from him. He turned on the light, but sat quietly, encouraging himself to get up. He couldn't believe this was happening to him. His emotions were so mixed. He closed his eyes and covered his face with his hands. Tears were rolling down his face. He placed one hand over his stomach as the aching increased. Eventually, he stood, wiped his face, and grabbed his phone that lay on the dresser beside his bed. He knew Alana was hungry, but didn't want her to ask any questions that would cause him to break. Therefore, he placed an order at the closest Italian restaurant. After placing the order, he fell onto the bed. Drew was drained.

Thirty minutes later, Alana knocked on the door. "Someone is at the door, Daddy!"

Drew awakened, grabbing his money as he walked towards the door. Alana clapped as she smelled the fresh garlic when Drew opened the door. After paying the driver, Drew made a plate for Alana.

"Are you going to eat?"

"I'm not really hungry, Babe. I'm too tired to eat. But, I will stay in here with you as you eat your food."

Alana kicked her feet back and forth, excited about spending time alone with her father.

"When is Mommy coming home?"

"I'm not sure."

Drew laid his head on the table. He tried to stay awake.

"Daddy, you must have had a long day at work! You can't stay awake!"

"I know."

Drew stood to grab a sheet of paper. He knew that this would be a great time to write. In the center of the page, he wrote "First Day".

For twenty minutes, he stared at the paper, writing nothing as Alana finished her meal. He stood to grab another sheet. He then wrote, "Every Day without You". Alana had finished her meal, washed her face and hands, and headed back to her room to play. Drew began to write:

My first day without you, what can I say,
I came home to find that all of your things had been taken away,
There was a note on the bed that caused my heart to break,
I asked God over and over, "What mistake did I make",

What could I have done to make you walk out of our life?
What could I have done better to keep my wife?
What about our daughter? Did you ask how she would feel?
How could you walk away from her? I can't believe this is real.

Where did you go? How could this be?
Today, we should be celebrating our anniversary.

Drew stopped writing. For ten minutes, he leaned back in his chair, staring at nothing. He stood, and placed the dishes in the dishwasher after washing them off. Then, he headed to the room.

Again, Drew started writing:

> We live this life once,
> So, why does there have to be,
> Another day without you,
> Are you not thinking about me?
>
> The times that we have shared,
> What do they mean to you?
> Would you not miss those days?
> Does this not make you feel blue?
>
> If I died tomorrow,
> Would you regret not coming around?
> Would you think of the times we shared,
> As they lay me in the ground?
>
> How could you be without me?
> We vowed until death do us part,
> Does this not feel like death to you?
> Is this not breaking your heart?

Drew stopped writing. He closed his eye, wondering what Salida was doing at that very moment. On Wednesday mornings, she usually awakened early to style her hair. She used to attend bible study every Wednesday, and never wanted the church goers to witness a bad hair day for her. He loved the fact that Wednesday and Sunday were the only two days that her hair ever mattered to her. On other days she would awaken to style her hair, but she always made sure that she was well kept for church. Wednesdays are also the days she didn't work out much, if at all. She'd spend most of her time lounging, reading, or baking for the restaurant.

The time was 4:57 p.m., and Bible study started at 7. He decided that he and Alana would be there, waiting to see if Salida would attend the service. He'd take her to the children's class as normal, and sit in their usual spot, waiting for Salida to walk in. Drew tried to prepare himself for what he knew would happen, but he couldn't help but hope that she would be there.

Their home was fifteen minutes away from the church. Drew made sure Alana's face and hands were clean. He walked her back to the class, greeted some of the other parents as usual, and headed to his seat. As church began, Drew felt a tightening in his stomach. Salida was always a couple of minutes late, but never more than ten minutes. Drew checked his watch. Fourteen minutes had gone by. Ten minutes later, he checked again. He looked around, checking to see if any of her friends from work were there. He noticed that Chelsea was sitting in the same spot in which she and Salida used to sit before he and Salida married. He decided he would ask her if she had seen Salida after church.

As church ended, he walked over to her. "Hi, how are you?"

"Fine, how are you?"

"I'm okay. Did Salida come to work today?"

"Noooo.... Salida actually quit working there about two weeks ago. She said that she had found another position somewhere else..... You're her husband. How come you're acting like you didn't know that?"

Drew swallowed hard, and turned to walk away.

"Do you not know where she is," asked Chelsea.

He continued walking towards the children's class. He grabbed Alana, thanked the teacher, and left. Drew realized that Salida had been planning to leave before she actually left. He strapped Alana into the car, and headed home.

Before he drove home, he decided to drive by her old home to see if she had been there. He thought the tenants would have seen her since the rent was due in two days. Three cars were in the driveway. Drew pulled up, cracked the windows a little, and got out of the car. He turned to Alana. "I'll be back in just a second. Stay here, and don't get out of your seat."

Alana nodded.

Drew walked to the house and knocked on the door. A man walked to the door with a curious look on his face.

"May I help you?"

"Yes, has Salida been over to collect the rent?"

"I'm not sure who Salida is."

"She's the lady that owns this home."

"No, we closed on this house about two months ago."

"You closed on the house two months ago?"

"Yes sir."

Drew was shocked. "I'm sorry for bothering you."

"Not a problem."

He walked back to the car, put it in reverse, and pulled out of the driveway. He wasn't sure where Salida was or how she was doing. He only knew that she had been planning her exit for quite some time. Drew tried to maintain his composure as he drove back to the house. He didn't want Alana to know what was going on.

As he pulled into the driveway, he thought about their account. After giving Alana a bath, and getting her ready for bed, he called to check the balance of their accounts. Drew found that Salida had taken more than half of their savings out of the account, and there was only $300 in their checking account. Luckily, he had opened another account after realizing that Salida had started to spend more. It wasn't as much as they had in their savings, but it was enough to get by for a little while. Plus, he was trying to save to purchase another vehicle. He was beginning to have problems with the car he had, and parting with it was necessary.

Drew couldn't believe that Salida had taken so much money. He walked to the room, got on his knees, and prayed. When he finished praying, he laid across the bed. Drew felt defeated. Before he fell asleep, he began to write:

Pain

God please come,
Take away all of this pain,
Being without her is like death,
I feel as if I'm going insane,

How could she walk out on us?
What did I do?
Were things that bad?
And I just never knew,

How come she never told me?
If something was wrong,
Could she not rely on me?
I thought our relationship was strong,

Yes, I knew something was wrong,
Money started leaving our account,
Just to go and buy lunch,
She'd take out a large amount,

I don't care about the money,
I just want my wife,
She was my queen, my beauty,
The love of my life,

God, please bring her back,
Please get rid of this strain,
Remove the knots in my stomach,
Relieve me of this pain.

Drew laid down his notebook, and slept. He awakened in the middle of the night, reaching for Salida. No comfort came to him when he realized that she wasn't there. Drew clenched his stomach, trying to control the pain that was in him. He thought about how carefully she had planned her exit, and was sickened by thought of her leaving him for someone else. He couldn't remember anything that he had done wrong. Again, Drew prayed. He needed answers, and no one, but God, could assist him. Eventually, Drew prayed himself back to sleep.

The next morning, he awakened to get Alana ready for daycare. He had no clue as to how to do her hair. Therefore, he brushed her hair into a ponytail. Then, he called his job to let them know that he wasn't coming in.
After getting Alana dressed, he rushed to the kitchen to prepare a small breakfast before he dropped her off. Alana sat on the other side of the table, kicking her feet back and forth and looking out the window as she ate.
"Daddy, where's mommy?"
"Mommy went on a trip. She'll be gone for a little while. Do you mind staying with Daddy?"
"Nope! You always make the best breakfast."
Drew managed to laugh at Alana's comment, "Thank you, Baby!"
Alana watched as Drew sat, never touching his food.
"Daddy, are you going to eat your food?"
"I will. I'm just not hungry right now."
"Okay, I'm just checking. My friend, Mia, loves to eat the breakfast that I don't eat."
"Is she in your Pre-K class?"
"Yes sir. Sometimes, I have to take my food with me when mommy is running late. So, when I'm full, Mia eats what's left."
Curiously, Andrew asked, "Why is mommy running late sometimes?"

"Sometimes, the guy that cuts our grass comes over really early in the morning. He always talks to mommy for a long time. So, I go in my room, and play while I'm waiting on them."

"Oh..... How come you've never talked to me about the guy that cuts the grass?"

"I don't know. I guess I haven't thought about it until now. He cuts the grass all of the time, almost every day!"

"Have you seen him cutting the grass?"

"No sir. But, I know he cuts the grass. His clothes are always dirty, and mommy told me that he cuts our grass."

Andrew sat, listening to Alana talk about their grass-cutter. He became more and more disgusted as she talked.

"So, has he ever talked to you?"

"Just a little."

"Did he tell you his name?"

"I call him, Mr. Jon."

"What does your mommy call him?"

Alana sat, thinking. "I don't remember."

"Okay...we have to get you to daycare. I have a few errands to run, and I don't want you to be late... By the way, I'm not that hungry. So, you can give my food to Mia."

Alana smiled, showing all of her teeth, "Thanks, Daddy!"

"No problem."

Drew took Alana to daycare. Anger had risen in him as he drove, thinking about the times Salida had called him to talk as he drove to work, wondering if she only called to make sure he wasn't returning home to catch her and "Mr. Jon" in the act.

Breaking Point

Andrew has been working for the same company for the past seven years. He enjoys what he does, but doesn't care for the management there. Although they'll never admit it, there are limitations for people that look like him. Yes, they may give some kind of lead position. But, to apply for a management or top-of-the-line position, one would have to be kidding. You could get written up for applying. An educational background, past

117

experience, etc. means nothing. It's all about the color of your skin, and the people that live in your neighborhood.

Happiness also seems to be a problem at this place. To smile in the midst of a stressful situation means that either you're not doing your job or you're not dedicated to your job.

His job is very stressful. Andrew put a photo of Alana on the desk to reassure himself of what makes him happy. Every time he looks at her, he smiles. He knows that what he does is temporary, and not in vain.

Since Salida had left, it's been harder for him to work over to stay caught up with the accounts he reconciles. At any time that he is able, he works over to catch up on work. This is not good enough for his manager.

His manager's name is Fabio Bradley Southerland. He goes by Bradley. Many are really starting to wonder if his mom should have named him BS or Full of BS. Fabio has a manager named Daniel Fakkas. He's just a whack as Bradley. The difference is that Daniel pretends to be holy, until you upset him. Then, he turns into Satan, always increasing your work load, altering your work percentage to decrease you incentive, watching you like a hawk to find ways to attack you.

There were numerous, educated, black people that were employed there. Drew noticed that, often, many of them would train the new hires. They would also take on some of the management duties. But, they were never given the opportunity to actually become managers, or given credit for their work. Many quit or moved on to other places of employment for that reason.

The issue of diversity was noticed throughout the company. Drew began to spend more of his break time with newer and older employees that looked like him to see what their view was regarding the issue. Often, without ever asking, their view was the same. He also noticed that most of the trainers were black women. These women would spend much of their day training, but were also pressured to have all of their work completed each day while training. Because of this, the door was constantly revolving.

It was January 8th, the cold temperature was hitting hard. May adults and children were getting sick. Drew had taken off one day because Alana wasn't feeling well. He called his manager to inform him of the situation.

"Thank you for calling. This is Bradley."

"Bradley, this is Andrew. My daughter is sick. So, I won't be able to make it in."

"No problem, family is first, you know?"

"I know. You know how I hate not coming in."

"It's okay. I know that when you take off, things are pretty serious. You're always here."

"Yeah, I know.... Well, I have to get back to her. Hopefully, I'll be in tomorrow."

"Okay, I'll see you then."

"Alright. Bye!

While Alana slept, Drew decided to log into the company's website to see if other positions were available.

He had a degree in Finance, and a Financial Analyst position had opened. There was also a position as a trainer for his department. A Budget Analyst and several other positions had also opened in some of the other buildings that were affiliated with the company. He applied for all of them, wanting to see if things had changed.

He also checked other websites to see if other positions were available. Before Alana had awakened, Drew had applied for over twenty positions. Completing applications exhausted Drew. Therefore, he decided that he would lie down after checking on Alana.

Alana wasn't feeling any better. Her eyes and nose were running at the same time. Drew grabbed tissue and a warm towel to clean her face. He gave her more medicine, picked her up, and took her to his bedroom. He lied down beside her.

Alana smiled; glad to be in the bed beside her father, certain that he was going to take care of her. Both drifted into a deep sleep, not waking for two hours.

After Drew had awakened, he called Tamara.

"Drewskey, what's up?"

"Not much. Alana is sick. I'm not sure what else to do as I have to work tomorrow."

"Do you need me to come up there?"

"That's a long drive, but I'm sure she won't be able to go to school tomorrow either. Will you able to come the next day? I'll take off tomorrow."

"I can come, tomorrow, after work if you need me."

"I really do need your help."

"Okay, I'll be there. Text me your address, and I'll be on my way as soon as I get off tomorrow."

"I really appreciate it."

"It's not a problem. I have six weeks of PTO time. I'm sure a few days won't hurt."

"Okay. Well, I'll chat with you when you get here."

"Alright, I will see you tomorrow night."

After hanging up with Tamara, Drew decided that he and Alana would go to the store to purchase more medicine. As he headed to the store, his car began to stall. After making it to the store, he popped the hood to see if his car was smoking, or if anything was leaking from his car. He didn't see anything. He and Alana walked into the store, grabbed the medicine, orange juice, and a few cans of soup. Then, they headed back to the car. As he headed back to the house, the car stalled again. After pulling into the garage, Drew sat for a while with his head down; frustrated with everything that was going on in his life. He looked back to check on Alana. She had drifted off to sleep again. Drew grabbed the bag of groceries, picked up Alana, and headed into the house. He called his manager to let him know that he wouldn't be in the following day either.

"This is Bradley. How may I help you?"

"Bradley, this is Drew again. My daughter isn't getting any better. I don't think I'll be in tomorrow either."

Bradley hesitated, "Are you behind on your work?"

"I'm not. I was up-to-date when I left the other day."

"Will you be able to catch up?"

"Of course I will. I have a friend that's going to come down the day after tomorrow to watch my daughter for me while I'm at work."

"You know, when you started here, we were assured that you would be able to make the sacrifices needed to complete your job in a timely manner. Not being here gets you behind."

"Bradley, I hardly ever take off, I have two hundred sixty-four PTO hours, and I'm not behind on my work. Why are we having this discussion?"

"We're having this discussion because you don't need to get behind on your work. It's hard enough when we all have to get together to help others get caught up."

"I understand that, but I also have responsibilities at home in which I have to take care of. Family is first."

"Well, I have to get back to work. I guess we will see you the day after tomorrow."

"I will be...."

Before Drew could finish his sentence, Bradley had hung up the phone.

"Bastard," Drew mumbled as he gritted his teeth. He had enough PTO hours to not come to work for weeks, and Bradley was giving him a hard time about two days. He couldn't believe it.

Drew was stressed. Salida left over six months ago, but he was still suffering from the circumstance. After she left, he had to take most of his money out of his savings to pay the daycare because of the money Salida had taken out of their checking account. He also found that she was weeks behind on paying the daycare. Therefore, he had to pay them for three weeks on top of the late fees they had incurred. Days ago, he had to use all, but ninety dollars of their joint savings to pay off a card that she had opened in his name. He immediately closed the card, and the account; pocketing the remaining ninety dollars. He also withdrew the three hundred dollars that was left in their checking account. The bills were also coming in because it was the beginning of the month. Drew called to pay those bills using a new checking account that he had opened at another bank. He had to take from his personal savings to cover those bills also. On top of that, he had to give Tamara gas money for coming to watch Alana. Drew was breaking. He didn't have enough money to buy another car. He couldn't afford to pay another babysitter. So, finding a second job wasn't an option. He didn't know what to do. He was already paying for aftercare at her school. Drew was weakened by the thought of the upcoming financial issues he would soon have.

Drew contacted one of his friends in search of a good auto mechanic, but his friend didn't have a specific mechanic. Then, he called his friend Joe.

"What's up Drew?"

"Not much, having a few issues with my car. So, I called to see if you know anyone that can take a look at it to tell me what I need to do to fix it."

"I do have one friend that can take a look at it."

"What's his name?"

"His name is Scott."

"Do you think he can look at it today?"

"I'm not sure. I can give you his number."

"Okay."

After contacting Scott, Drew was advised to bring his car in.

"It seems that one of your sensors is going bad on the car, causing it to stall a little when you're driving."

"Can you fix it for me?"

"I'm a little busy today. I'll have to order the part also."

"Can I drive it anyway?"

"I wouldn't recommend that you drive it too far. However, it's drivable. I have a guy that can deliver the part for me, I just need to work on a few other cars, and I'll let you know what I can do today."

"Please help me out. I am really trying to hang on to my job." He pointed to Alana that was in the back seat of the car, sleeping. "My daughter is sick. I have a friend that is coming tomorrow to help me out. I really need my car."
Drew's plea made Scott very sympathetic. "Hang on a minute."
Scott walked away to make a phone call. Drew sat quietly, watching his car. Moments later, Scott returned. "I think I can get you in today. I have already sent someone out to get the part. I'm waiting on another part for one of the other cars."
Drew let out a sigh of relief.
"Man, I know what it's like to have to stay home with the kids. I used to work for a company that wanted you there all of the time. I had to call out often because my son was always sick."
"Really?"
"Yeah, being around other kids never made him any better. You know how it is when you take your kids to school or daycare, and the other kids are sick. Your kid is likely to get whatever one of those other kids has."
"You're right."
"So, I decided to pursue this dream of being an auto mechanic. I've been working on cars with my father since I was about nine or so."
"That's pretty amazing."
"Where's her mom?"
Drew's heart seemed to have dropped. He swallowed hard. "She walked out on us some months ago."
"Wow, I'm sorry to hear that."
"It's okay. I've been doing my best to make things happen for the two of us since then. It hasn't been easy."
"I'm sure. I can't imagine what it's like to have to get up every morning, and try to get a little girl ready for school."
"Hey, I'm going to get her out of the car. She's not feeling well, but we haven't eaten yet."
"No problem. There are a few fast food places up the street if you feel like walking. There are also a few restaurants farther down the street that may have soup since your daughter is sick."
"Okay, we'll walk to get something. I'll try to call someone to come and get us... How long do you think it will take before you can finish working on the car?"
"It's going to be about six to seven hours. We have to make sure that everything is okay after we install the censor."
"Okay."

Drew called his friend Gerald that manages the night shift for a shipping company.

"What's up, Drew?"

"Hey man, I'm down the street from you, getting my car fixed. It's going to take a while for them to fix it, and my daughter is sick. I was wondering if you could take us back to the house."

"Not a problem. Let me get some clothes on, and I'll be on my way."

"Alright, I really appreciate it."

"It's not a problem."

Gerald showed up in no time at all. He was Drew's most reliable friend. He never complained, never asked a lot of questions, and never said "no" if there was ever a time that Drew needed him.

"Man, I really appreciate this."

"It's not a problem. I have to go in early today. I'll have my wife to come pick the two of you up when she gets off. The timing will be perfect since she has to pass by your area to get home."

"That's great! Man, you are a life saver."

"Drew, you never ask me for anything, you've always given me good advice, and you've always been there when I needed you. It's very rare for you to call me, needing anything. I can't say no to that. When I heard that your wife walked out, I told my wife, "She's a fool." Man, I couldn't believe that happened to you."

Drew remained silent as Gerald talked. He couldn't believe that this was happening to him either. He continued looking out of the window. His mind was blank. He didn't want to discuss any issues he was having with anyone, but God. He knew he had to pray.

After Gerald dropped the two of them off, Drew warmed the soup for Alana. Alana didn't eat much. She laid her head down on the table, and drifted. Drew picked her up, and laid her in her bed. After walking to his room, he got on his knees to pray:

"God, what have I done wrong? My child is sick, my wife left, my car is messed up, I have bills coming in left and right, my job is on the line, and my wife has been spending all of our money, probably with Mr. Jon. I'm at the bottom. I really need your help. Where are you? Please let me know that you see what's going on. I am drowning right now. My manager is not helping at all. All of my audits are 100%, I'm up-to-date on my balancing, and he's still giving me a hard time. He's even given me more work. How can that be when I'm past the maximum amount allowed for one person?"

Drew slid from the bed to the floor, onto his back. He folded his hands over his head and sighed.

"Lord, do you even hear me? Please, tell me what I'm doing wrong." He waited, looking around his room as if the answer was there. Drew felt a burning sensation in his heart. It had been there for a while. It was so heavy that it changed the way he walked.

Drew laid silently in the same spot, waiting on nothing.

An hour later, he called Tamara.

"Hey!"

"Hey, are you sure you can come tomorrow?"

"Actually, I might have to leave today."

"Really?"

"Yes, I received a call from a company there. They were willing to pay twice the amount of what I make here. So, I have an interview at eight. Afterwards, you can go in, and work the rest of the day."

Drew let out a sigh of relief.

Tamara continued, "Yeah, I'm going to claim that position. Once I get it, I will need somewhere to stay for a while."

"You can stay in the guestroom."

"Are you sure?"

"I'm positive."

"What about Salida? What if she returns?"

"Tam, I don't think Salida is coming back. She's not answering my calls or anything."

"Okay, well, I'll need somewhere to stay for a little while anyway. I need just enough time to find a nice spot."

"You're welcome to stay. I really need your help right now. You and I both know that I can't do Alana's hair."

Tamara laughed, "I know."

After hanging up with Tamara, Drew let out a sigh of relief. He felt that he was finally receiving a break.

Tamara arrived later that night. Drew was so excited to see her. He grabbed her bag from the car and showed her to the guestroom. He sighed, "I'm so glad you're here. I really need your help right now."

"It's not a problem. I'm glad to come and help. You know that. I don't have any kids of my own, but I can only imagine what it's like to have to work and raise one by yourself."

"Yeah, but you know that I never expected this to happen. Alana didn't ask for this either."

"I know." Tamara finally had a chance to take a long look at Drew. He looked horrible, as if he had been running a race only to find that the odds were always against him. Being that they grew up together, and were always best friends, she knew that she could express herself, "I can see that things aren't going so well for you. You look very fragile."

Drew agreed, "I've lost some weight, been under a lot of stress. I haven't been eating like I'm supposed to. I've had so much to happen in the past six months. Got my car fixed earlier today. That cost me a little bit. My manager also gave me a hard time about not being able to come in tomorrow. I have so much PTO time the he shouldn't have said anything. My child is sick. I had to pay off a card that Salida opened in my name. The aftermath of my marriage is killing me."

"Wow."

"That's just a portion of the things that I've been going through." Drew shook his head. "I can't win."

Tamara felt horrible. "Why didn't you call me before?"

"I thought that things would change. Every time I think that there's a breakthrough, I fall into another hole."

Tamara observed Drew for a moment. She had never seen this side of him. He looked malnourished, restless, and broken. "You know what? I'm going to stay the rest of the week to help you."

"You don't have to do that!"

"I want to. I'll stay here, and watch Alana while you go to work."

"Tam, you have a life of your own. You don't have to do this for me."

"Drew, you need a break, and I have the time. I'll watch Alana, while you go to work. I'm only missing two days of work anyway."

Drew hugged Tamara as hard as he could. "You are a life saver."

Tamara smiled, "Where's Alana?"

"She's asleep. She's been resting off and on all day."

"You should get some rest yourself. I'm going to go to the interview tomorrow. Then, I'll be back to take care of Alana." Tamara continued, "I'm really hoping that I get this job."

Drew agreed, "I hope so too. That will help me out a lot."

Tamara was getting sleepy, "Well, I'm going to take my shower, and go to sleep now."

Drew decided to get some rest also, "Good night."

"Good night."

Tamara closed the door to the guest room. She couldn't believe that Drew had reached such a low point in his life without reaching out to his family or friends. She didn't know many men that were as humble as Drew. To see that he was suffering in silence left her perplexed. She prayed for Drew, asking God to handle whatever problems he had.

Drew took a look at himself in the bathroom mirror. He knew that he looked bad, but Tamara's expression made things seem worse than he thought. Yes, he had missed a few meals, had discontinued working out at the gym, and needed to shave a little, but she distanced herself from him as if he wasn't the same person. He decided that he would get up early in the morning and shave his face before heading to work.

The next day, Drew awakened just in time to shave and cook breakfast for Tamara before she headed off to her interview. Tamara was excited about eating Drew's breakfast, "Boy, you know that you can cook!"
Drew laughed, "I haven't cooked for you in a very long time."
Tamara agreed, "I know. I miss those donuts you used to make when we were growing up."
"You know, I haven't made those donuts in years, probably not since we were young."
"Why?"
"I don't know. Just haven't thought of it."
"What about the quesadillas you used to make for everyone?"
"I make those from time to time."
"Those were so good!"
"I'll make some tonight. I added a new flavor to them. So, I know you'll really like them now."
"Yes! I can't wait!" She checked the time, "I have to go now! I'll see you whenever I get back!"
"See you later."
Tamara left as if she was in a hurry. Her interview was only ten minutes away, and she had an hour to get there.
After Tamara left, Drew fixed a plate for Alana. He entered her room to find that she was still asleep.
Softly, Drew said, "Hey, Babe."
Alana reached out for him, "Daddy." She was extremely congested, her eyes were watery, and she looked helpless. Drew hated seeing her that way. "Sit up so that you can eat some breakfast."
"I'm not hungry."

"You have to eat. If you don't eat, you won't feel better. I also brought you some orange juice and medicine. You will have to blow your nose before you can eat, or you won't be able to taste anything."

Alana sat up slowly, and cleaned her nose. She took a couple of sips of orange juice, and began to eat the food on her plate. "Daddy, can you sit with me?"

"Sure, but only for a little while. My friend, Tamara, is here to watch you while I go to work. Can you be a good girl for me?"

"Is that your friend that we see when we go to your hometown?"

"Yes."

"She's pretty and very nice."

Drew agreed, "Yes, she is."

"I will be good."

"I know you will." Drew checked the time on his phone, "I have to shower for work. I'll be back after I get ready. Can you finish all of your breakfast for Daddy?"

"Yes sir."

"Good girl. I'll be back in a minute."

The timing was perfect. Drew had finished washing dishes, and was ready for work when Tamara returned. "How did the interview go?"

Tamara smiled, "I think it went well."

"So, what did they say?"

"He seemed a little impressed."

"It was a man?"

"Yes."

"You probably got the job."

"What does that mean?"

"Nothing, just saying you probably got it."

Tamara threw the kitchen towel at Drew. "I know what you're trying to say!"

Drew laughed. "Hey, Alana has eaten, and is sleep again. She probably won't wake up for a while. I also gave her some medicine. You can give her more around noon or so. There's food in the refrigerator. Eat whatever you'd like. I'm going to head out."

"Okay, no problem. By the way, I know how you are. Do not call here every hour to see if things are okay. Alana and I will be fine."

Drew smiled, "You're a life saver!"

Tamara shook her head, "Get out of here!"

Bradley approached Drew's desk five minutes after Drew arrived. "I thought that you needed the day off?"

"One of my friends is at the house, watching my daughter until I get off."

Bradley frowned, "What kind of friend?"

Drew never stopped working to look at Bradley, "A close friend."

"I checked your report yesterday. You're not behind. So, missing another day wouldn't have been a problem."

Drew didn't respond. He worked as fast as he could to get ahead of himself. Eventually, Bradley walked away, but observed Drew's report off and on over the next eight hours.

Drew called Tamara during his breaks and lunch to see how Alana was doing. Tamara fussed at him every time, but she was certain that he wouldn't stop. Those were the only times that Drew wasn't working. He was excited about how much work he had done to get ahead, and knew there would be hardly anything for him to do the next day.

As he headed home, he tried to remember whether or not he had everything necessary to make the quesadillas and a few side items. He stopped by the store to get some tomatoes and tortillas. As soon as he stepped out of his car, he noticed Jonathan and Salida walking through the parking lot. Neither of them saw him. Salida's smile guaranteed that she was happy being with Jonathan. Drew said nothing to the couple as he no longer needed an explanation. He walked into the store, grabbed the things he needed, and left.

Tamara sat at the kitchen table, grinning from ear to ear when Drew walked in. "What are you so happy about?"

"I got the job!"

Drew chuckled, "That is great!"

For a moment, she jumped around the kitchen like a kid. "So, how was work?"

"It was the same."

Even in her excitement, she could sense that something was wrong. "Something is bothering you. What is it?"

Drew shook his head.

"That's not true, Drew."

Drew almost hated that she knew him so well. "I'm going to check on Alana."

Tamara grabbed his arm. "Please don't hold your feelings inside like this. We've been best friends all of our life."

Drew turned to her, "I just don't want to talk about it. Today has been a good day for you."

"Not when my friend isn't happy."

Drew managed an awry smile, and Tamara let go of his arm. He walked to the room to check on Alana. As soon as he stepped into the room, Alana hugged his leg, "Hi, Daddy!"

Tamara watched as Alana seemed to change Drew's demeanor. He picked her up, "How are you feeling?"

"I feel better."

"You look and sound better!"

"Yes sir, Mrs. Tamara rubbed this stuff on my chest. I can breathe better now."

"That's great!"

"She also helped me comb my dolls' hair. It was a mess!"

Drew laughed, "I would have loved to have seen that!" Tamara folded her arms. Drew continued, "What else did she do?"

"We had soup for lunch, and watched a movie. Then, she combed my hair."

"It's very pretty."

"Thanks, Daddy!"

"You're welcome. I'm going to let you play a little while longer while I start on dinner."

Tamara interceded, "Well, since you were working, and I was here, I cooked dinner."

Drew smiled, "So, that's what I smelled when I walked in!"

"Yep!"

"I bought tomatoes and tortillas to make the quesadillas."

"You can make them tomorrow or something."

"Okay." Drew headed towards the kitchen, "I can't remember the last time I came into my kitchen to eat someone else's cooking."

"Are you serious?"

"Yes."

"Is that why you're so scrawny?"

Drew frowned, "I'm not scrawny."

"Drew, you've lost a lot of weight. I was really worried about you for a minute."

He agreed, "I know."

"Have you talked to your family?"

"Off and on, not like I usually do."

"Why?"

"Just not ready to tell them that she left."

"It's been over six months and they still don't know?"

"Other than the people that live here, you are the only one that knows."

"Why are you doing this to yourself?"

Drew sat at the table, watching as Tamara added the plates and silverware. He held his head down, "My father never wanted me to marry Salida."

"Why?"

"He just knew that something wasn't right with her. He told me that when he first met her, but I always knew that my father wanted me to marry someone else. So, I didn't listen."

"Mr. D wouldn't hold that against you. He's your father! He loves you, and wants the best for you."

"Well, I thought that she would return before I let him know that she had left."

"Have you even talked to her?"

"No." He contemplated on telling her that he had seen her not more than an hour ago, but decided against it. He knew that she would have more questions. He decided to change the conversation. "So, when will you start your new job?"

"I have to put in my two weeks' notice. Then, I'll start."

"That's great."

She thought for a moment, "Are you sure that you're okay with me staying here for a while until I find somewhere to stay?"

"I'm positive! Honestly, I really need you here right now. Things have been falling apart for me lately, and I don't have anyone else to rely on that wouldn't hold it against me."

Tamara was very sympathetic, but didn't want to show it. She began to place the food on the table. "Let's eat before the food gets cold."

"Okay." Drew ran to get Alana so that the three of them could eat at the same time.

Tamara left that Saturday morning. She wanted to get home to write out her resignation letter, and wash clothes. Although she hated to admit it, she really enjoyed the small amount of time that she had spent with Drew and Alana. Alana was beautiful, respectful, and profoundly innocent. Her love for her father was undeniable. Tamara realized that at the present time, Alana was the only person that gave Drew some peace of mind.

Alana also hated to see Tamara leave. Tamara's presence brought life to the house after Salida had left. She hadn't seen her father happy and talking for months until Tamara had come. She asked Drew, "Why did Ms. Tamara have to leave?"

"She came here to watch you while you were sick, but she'll be back in a couple of weeks. Then, she's going to stay for a while until she can find somewhere else to stay."

"Why can't she just stay here?"

Drew knew that Alana wouldn't understand. However, he tried to explain, "She's a really, good friend of mine, but she has a life of her own. I'm sure she's going to want some privacy at some point in time."

"She has a door to her room. When I want to play by myself, I close the door."

"I know, sweetie. It's a little different when you're grown."

Alana didn't respond. Instead, she headed back to her room to play with her dolls.

Drew walked to his room to write. He realized that his writing decreased when Tamara was present. He assumed that conversing with her gave him no reason to write about the things that bothered him. Therefore, the only time that he took out his notebook to write was when she was asleep. As he sat in his room, he thought of the glow in Salida's eyes as she walked away from the store with Jonathan. He realized that he hadn't seen that glow in years. He thought of how wholesome she looked as the two of them walked towards his SUV. *She always loved him,* he thought to himself. Drew's stomach began to churn all over again. He, then, wrote a poem that he named I Saw You. When he finished, he added it to the folder.

Drew knew that God had been calling him to his purpose. Although he knew it, he tried to ignore the feeling. However, that same feeling stayed with him at all times, causing anxiety to kick in when he was working. He knew he didn't belong there. At night he would awaken, unsure of what he was supposed to be doing at that time. Therefore, he wrote. He wrote about the feelings he had, he wrote about the times that he would awaken, and he wrote about the things that he saw in his dreams. He wasn't even certain that they were dreams, at times he was half asleep, and they came. On this particular night, Drew dreamed of surrender. Promptly, he awakened as he didn't want to forget what he had seen. Drew began to write:

Here I am, Lord,
I'm lonely and I feel lost,
To ignore what you have called me to do,

I never counted up the cost,

I can't run anymore,
Been sitting in this wilderness with no direction,
I have to rely on you alone,
God, you're my only protection,

All kinds of animals are surrounding me,
I can see their eyes, but cannot fight,
I remain still because it's so dark,
God, you're my only light,

In this wilderness, I feel that I've lost my strength,
I feel so weak and I can't eat,
You never let me down, nothing consumes me,
The relationship I have with you, no one can compete,

The longer that I'm in this place,
The more I am able to rely solely on you,
I feel this ever-so-amazing peace,
My heart, my soul, I feel so anew,

In the darkest areas, I'm comforted more,
As I walk along the path in this place,
I get tired, but you encourage me,
Oh, how I'm moved by your grace,

God, you are so awesome,
You're my provider, my father, my friend,
At times, when I get to the end of the tunnel,
I long to return to the wilderness again.

Drew let out a sigh. His writings brought him so much relief. He took his poem, and added it to his folder.

Over the next two weeks, Drew dedicated one hour to cleaning up the house and making sure that everything was in place. He didn't want anything out of pocket when Tamara arrived. She had called three days before her arrival to state that she would be there Saturday as she wanted to unpack her things, and go out to eat later on that night to celebrate her new job. Drew had also advised her to not tell the family that she was moving in with him. She agreed.

Drew received a bonus on his last paycheck that helped out a lot. Because he didn't want Tamara to have to style Alana's hair when the three of them went out, he took her to the hairdresser. After leaving, he took her to get a dress. Alana tried on several dresses before Drew finally decided on one. He loved them all, but the one that he had chosen matched the attire that he had set out for the night.

Tamara arrived two hours after Drew and Alana had returned to the house. As soon as she stepped through the door, Alana ran to hug her. Tamara dropped her boxes as if she was about to hug a friend that she hadn't seen in years.

"You look so nice! Look at your hair."

"Thank you! Daddy took me to get my hair done today. He said that I couldn't mess it up because I had to be cute for tonight."

Tamara laughed, "Well, you are cute every day."

Alana smiled, "I can help you unpack if you want me to. Daddy showed me how to fold my clothes so that all of them will fit in my drawers neatly."

"Awe, that's sweet, but my clothes are already folded. I made sure that they were nice and neat before I put them in boxes. The clothes that are in bags are clothes that I need to put on a hanger."

"Okay."

Drew entered the room, and noticed the boxes scattered about. "I didn't know you had boxes. I'll help you get them."

"It's okay. They're not heavy. I brought in my underclothes first. My other clothes are still in the car in bags."

"I'll go and get those."

Drew headed out the door to grab the bags, while Tamara and Alana took the boxes in her room. He advised Alana to give Tamara time to get her things together. Then, the three of them would head out.

Tamara loved the guestroom. It was much larger than her previous room. She had lived in a one bedroom, studio apartment. It was only 600 square feet. Drew's guestroom also had its own bathroom, which made Tamara like it even more. As soon as she finished unpacking, she showered. She didn't want them to wait too long to eat.

Drew had advised her to wear something nice. Therefore, she grabbed a dress that dazzled along with a nice pair of heels. Tamara wasn't used to the attire, but she needed it for the occasion. She knew that Drew loved to look nice. Therefore, she wanted to look impressive. That, she did. Drew's mouth seemed to have dropped as she stepped out of the room.

Tamara asked as she spun around, "What do you think?"

Alana smiled, "You look really pretty!"

Drew added, "I don't think I've seen you in a dress since our twelfth grade prom."

"Do you think I'm overdressed?"

"Absolutely not, you look great!"

"Well, quit looking at me like that! You're making me nervous!"

Alana laughed. Drew replied, "I'm just shocked to that you look like that in a dress! I've always seen you in pants!"

Tamara grabbed her jacket, "Let's go."

Drew had reserved a spot at one of the most expensive restaurants in the city. He knew that it was pricey, but he figured that he owed this to all of them as he and Alana hadn't been out for a while, and Tamara wouldn't accept money from him. Alana stood in awe as she saw the gold lights that were on the trees inside the building. To her, it was Christmas all over again. As they stood in the lobby, watching Alana, someone said, "Do you have reservations?"

Drew stepped up, "Yes, Davison is the last name."

With arrogance in his voice, the greeter said, "Walk this way, please."

As the three of them followed the greeter, many heads turned in dismay as if they had stepped into the wrong restaurant. Drew also noticed that several tables were available in the front. However, they were directed to a corner in the farthest area away from everyone else. He said nothing as he didn't want to spoil the meal.

Alana asked, "Daddy, why are we sitting all the way back here?"

"I'm not sure. I guess the other seats were reserved for someone else."

Afterwards, a waitress arrived. Wide-eyed and seemingly shocked by their presence, she asked, "How are you all today?"

Drew answered, "We're doing well?"

"That's great! Would you like something to drink for starters?"

"Yes, I would like a sprite for my daughter." He looked at Tamara, "Would you like something to drink?"

"Yeah, I'll have Sangria."

The waitress added, "That's a nice choice! What would you like to drink, sir?"

"I would like Riesling."

"We also have Crown and Coke or Gin and Juice. We try to cater to everyone."

Drew and Tamara both lowered their menus to take a look at the waitress. "Riesling it is." She began to step away, but turned back, "I know that some of our menu items are a little pricey. So, if you would like to share a meal we can bring out three plates for you."
Drew balled his fist under the table.
Tamara replied, "Thank you!" Swiftly, the waitress walked away.
Drew sat silently, staring at the menu, but also wanting to walk out of the restaurant. He realized that this was probably the reason why no one ever insisted that he eat dinner at this place. He didn't see anything on the menu that seemed to be any different from any other place he had eaten anyway.
Tamara asked, "Do you want to leave? I don't see anything on the menu that I want. Plus, I don't care for the atmosphere."
"I do want to leave."
"Okay, let's go."
The three of them left, certain that they would never return to that restaurant again.
As they entered the car, Drew apologized for taking them there.
Tamara responded, "It's not your fault. None of us expected to deal with anything like that."
Drew considered taking Tamara and Alana to the place with the fire pits. He knew that Alana would love it. "I have something else in mind." The place was only six minutes way.
They loved it. Alana and Tamara couldn't believe that although they were sitting outside, they were still warm because of the fire pits. Tamara said, "Drew, this place is nice!"
Alana agreed, "Yes, I like the fireplaces, Daddy!"
Drew smiled, "The food is good, and the service is great too!"
Tamara sat, unable to decide on what she would like to eat.
Drew asked, "Do you want me to order for you?"
"Sure."
"Okay, there's a dish here that I know you will love."

After dinner, the three of them headed home. Tamara placed her hand over her stomach, "That food was amazing!"
Drew smiled. "I'm glad you liked it."
Alana had fallen asleep after stuffing herself.
Tamara added, "I can't wait to taste the dessert that you bought from there!"
"You'll love it too. I would ask you to take a bite, but I can almost promise you that you won't stop eating it."

"Yeah, I don't need that right now. My stomach already feels as if it's about to explode."

Drew laughed, "You have no stomach, that's why it feels that way."

"I do. It's just not as large as some others."

"Whatever."

As soon as they entered the house, Tamara locked the door to the guestroom, removed her clothes, and fell across her bed. Drew carried Alana to her bedroom, removed her shoes and dress, and struggled to get her nightgown on her. He, then, headed to his own room. He was so glad that the night turned out well after leaving the first restaurant. The look on everyone's face as they were directed to their table, how they were seated in the farthest corner of the restaurant, and the words of the waitress played in his head over and over again. He also thought of how no one ever called him for an interview after he applied for over twenty positions. He considered the fact that he was the only one in his department that had a degree in Finance, but his manager wouldn't give him a lead position. He stretched out over his bed, and began to write:

Color

Why am I not growing with this company?
I have seven years in,
My major disadvantage is the color of my skin,

My manager has no degree,
I'm the one that went to college,
I've scored 100% on every audit,
It can't be that I'm lacking knowledge,

I'm tired of being mistreated by them,
God, you know this is not right,
You assured me that you would handle this,
I understand this is not my fight,

When will I see the sign?
Will I get a chance to see them fail?
Some days I want to pack my things,

And tell them all to go to hell,

Instead, I come in every day,
Sitting at my desk, I wear my mask,
To grin and hide my disapproval,
It's such a difficult task,

How can they discriminate against me?
Before our meetings, they shake my hand,
They look for me in search of an answer,
For everything that they don't understand,

When I have a question for them,
The answer is never clear,
Usually, they just say that they don't know,
I want to ask, "Why are you here?"

The discrimination is undeniable,
It's written on every face,
For every meeting that I've attended,
There's never been a manager of my race,

The next time a position opens,
Let's be fair to one another,
Choose the person because of what they know,
Not because their skin is a certain color.

After finishing his poem, Drew placed it in a new folder. He hadn't named
it, but he was certain that he had something in the making.

Tamara had been watching Alana catch the bus to school for months now.
She loved doing it, but felt that she was ruining her welcome with Drew.
She had also become attracted to a guy that she had met while working out
at the gym. She was certain that it was disrespectful to bring someone into
the house like that. Therefore, she knocked on the door to Drew's bedroom
to discuss the issue.
"Come in."

She pushed the door open, "You're always in your room. What are you usually doing when you're in here?"

"Nothing, just watching television. Sometimes I'll read. What's up?"

"I wanted to talk to you for a minute." She sat on the bed. "I love being with you guys. Alana is an amazing girl but, I kind of feel as if I'm ruining my welcome."

"Why do you feel that way?"

"I'm always here. Plus, I have met someone that I'm really interested in, but I can't bring him here."

"Can you not go to his place to visit him?"

"If you met someone, and you told her that you live with your best friend and her child, how do you think she would feel?"

"I understand that," Drew continued, "but, if you leave, I'll have to change my schedule, and start paying for aftercare again. I've been able to save that money for other things. That's two hundred dollars out of my pocket every month for them to watch my child for two hours after school."

"What if I continue to come over in the mornings to make sure that she catches the bus?"

Drew sat at the end of the bed, quite disgusted with his response, "I'm sorry. I'm being selfish. Alana is not your responsibility. I needed your help, and you came to help me. You've done more than enough, and I truly appreciate it. Do whatever you want to do. You have a life of your own, no kids, no responsibilities.... I understand."

For just a moment, Tamara thought of leaving Alana. She had become so drawn to her. She thought of coming into an empty house, and no one is waiting on her. Now, every day that she comes in, Drew has cooked, and Alana has her arms wrapped around her. She stood, "Never mind. I'm sorry that I even brought it up."

Drew grabbed her arm, "Seriously, Tam. Don't stay here because of me. I was being selfish."

"I'm not staying here because of you."

"Then, why did you say never mind?"

"No reason. You're right. I can go to his house when I want to see him."

"Just seconds ago you were certain that you were ready to leave."

She sat down on the bed beside Drew, "I do want to date this guy. I'm attracted to him and everything, but I can't leave Alana."

Drew sat in dismay. "Are you serious? You've never liked kids."

"I know. For some reason, I'm drawn to her. I was just thinking of what life would be like when I come home, and she's not there. Every time I walk through this door, she runs to greet me as if she's been waiting on me all day. No one makes me feel as important and needed as she does, not my family, not the people at work, no one. She hugs me and tells me that she loves me every day before she gets on the bus. When she gets on it, she waves and waves as if I'm the only person that she sees. I love it. I feel that if I walk away from her, she'll think that everyone will." Tamara continued, "I even have pictures of us on my desk. Everyone thinks that she's my child."

Drew shook his head, "How did you become so attached to her?"

Tamara held her head down, "I don't know. We go to the park and the arcade, we get ice cream, and she helps me pick out clothes at the mall..... Maybe it's because we do so much together."

"What do you want to do?"

"I'll stay. Maybe if I help out on some of the bills, things will be easier for you."

"That's not fair."

"Yes, it is. If I help with some of the bills, I won't feel as if I'm freeloading."

"You're not. I asked you to stay here."

Tamara stood to walk away. She didn't want to argue with Drew about her wanting to pay. Instead, she decided that she would deposit money into his account every month. She knew which bank he used, and was sure that he wouldn't hand her the money if he wasn't sure who was depositing it.

Salida was sitting at her desk, looking at pictures of herself and Alana. She missed her deeply, but was afraid that Drew would refuse to let her see Alana because she had walked out on them. She knew that Alana caught the bus every morning around seven thirty. She decided to use one of the company's cars, and sit at a distance to watch her get on the bus the next day.

As she flipped through the pictures, she ran across a photo of her and Jonathan in Italy. She became angry with herself for falling for him. She truly enjoyed the trip to Italy, and thought that things would get better for the two of them, only to find that he only needed someone that he could sleep with from time to time. He wouldn't even let her move in with him as he had stated that he needed time alone. Before she walked out on Drew and Alana, he seemed certain that they belonged together, and insisted that he wanted another child with her. Now, he only calls when he's short on funds, or needs sex.

The next morning, she arrived five minutes early. She sat across the street, waiting for Drew to rush Alana out to catch the bus. She became furious when she saw Tamara walking out of the house with Alana. Her anger increased when Alana wrapped her arms around Tamara right before she stepped onto the bus. She sped off, grabbed her phone, and, without thinking, began to call Drew.

Bewildered by her call, Drew answered, "Hello."

"What the hell is Tamara doing at our house?"

"Hold on. I have to step away from my desk."

Salida waited. She could hear Drew's steps as he headed towards the door.

"Okay."

"Drew, why is she there?"

He started to answer her, but considered his options. "You walked out on us, and now you're calling to ask why another woman is helping me take care of my daughter?"

"It's Tamara! I knew that she wanted to be with you! How long has she been there?"

"Why were you driving by the house?"

"Are you going to answer me?"

"She found a job here, and I was about to lose mine. So, I asked her to stay at the house to help me."

Salida sat on the other end, saying nothing as she realized all of the chaos she had caused.

"Hello?"

Salida replied, "I'm still here."

"Are you going to answer my question?"

"I drove by, hoping to see that the two of you were doing well without me. When I saw Alana wrap her arms around Tamara, I got mad. I know I shouldn't have. Drew, I really miss you and Alana."

"Salida, you've created such a mess in my life, I'm not even sure that I want to see you right now."

"I know I did. I'm sorry, but I needed to get away for a while. Things have been a bit of a mess for me. Sometimes, I want to call you, but...."

"I can't talk for a long time. I have to get back to work."

"Can we meet or something?"

"Why?"

"I want to talk to you. Just for a little while. You can come over if you want."

"Where do you live?"

"2305 Steward Circle"

"Okay, I'll come over when Tamara gets home."

"Okay."

Drew hung up.

When Tamara came in from work, Drew left. He called Salida to advise that he was on his way.

"Hello?"

"Hey, are you home?"

"Yes."

"I'm almost in your neighborhood. Can you open the door?"

"Okay, I just unlocked the door."

Drew pulled into the parking space, and headed towards the door. Salida waited behind the door with nothing on. As soon as Drew opened the door, she grabbed him pulling him to her. Drew pushed her away. She turned to him.

"What's wrong? Why'd you stop me?"

"I thought that you wanted to talk. Otherwise, I shouldn't be here."

"Why?"

"This doesn't better things for us. Coming over and sleeping with you just says that I accept you not being at home."

He opened the door to leave.

"Drew, wait a minute. Where are you going to go?"

"I'm going home."

"Are you going to be with her?"

Annoyed, Drew said, "Do you know how many people I can just sleep with? It takes no energy. Women are always throwing themselves out there. I have never shared myself with anyone the way that I shared myself with you. I have also explained that Tamara and I are just friends. I came here because I wanted to see my wife."

Salida held her head down. "I don't deserve that title, nor do I deserve you."

"I agree, but it doesn't stop me from loving you, Salida." Drew closed the door, and headed home.

When entering his house, he walked straight to his room. Drew began to write:

Tired

I've had enough,
I've loved so much,
I miss your heart,

I miss your touch,

How long do I wait?
For someone who,
Plays with my heart,
And makes me feel blue,

Do you not feel just like me?
Do you wonder why this has to be?

I've waited long,
The love has not died,
To rid myself of this feeling,
I promise I've tried,

Love suffers long,
It's not puffed up,
God, please take this from me,
I want another cup,

A cup of joy,
No more pain in my heart,
Please provide a new cup,
I'm ready for a fresh start,

Someone that loves hard,
And makes me feel free,
That loves you just as much,
And worships you with me,

One that's chosen by you,
That cherishes life and loves to see,
All of the beautiful things that you've created,
While sharing that time with me.

Drew sighed as he finished. He stored the poem in the folder with all of the other poems he had written. Drew was tired. He had waited so long for Salida to return, to love him as if they had never been apart. He picked up his pen, and began to write again.

Drew dreaded going to work the next day. He knew there had to be more for him. Every day he prayed, asking God for clarity on why the color of his skin was such an issue, why could no one see his ability based on his skills and education alone? He prayed for purity, and the ability to work in an environment where he and others had the same objective, to get the job done, accurately and in a timely manner. Drew's anxiety grew like weeds that fed on the richest soil, and his motivation for working constantly decreased.

While working, he spent most of his time, trying to think of what he could do to get out of his situation. He thought of returning to school, applying for other positions within the company, or just leaving the company completely. At the time, none of the options sound feasible.

When he wasn't working, he spent most of his time at the park with Alana. At other times, he would hang out with a few of his friends.

Drew's sleep pattern had also changed. He'd written an "Every Day without You" poem every night before bed, and other poems throughout the day. His folder had just about taken all that it could take. Lately, at around two o'clock, Drew would awaken, and had a very hard time going back to sleep. He tossed and turned for hours when trying. It was Monday morning, at four when Drew looked towards the ceiling, and said, "God, you're so loud. I can't go back to sleep because you keep calling me. The problem is that I'm not sure what it is that I'm supposed to be doing. Can you give me some assistance?" Drew lay back down, and ended his conversation in Jesus' name. Finally, he dozed.

The next night, after finishing his poem, he dozed. But, again, he awakened in the middle of the night. He grabbed his pillow, and covered his head, but he still couldn't sleep. At times, he would doze, but awaken minutes later. He grabbed his phone to check the time. It was 3:07. He sat up in the bed. His mind wandered for a while. He thought of the dreams he'd had lately. Minutes had gone by, but Drew couldn't go back to sleep. He decided to start on another poem:

Loud

God, I hear you calling,
Your voice is so loud,
It's 3:30 in the morning,
My mind is in a cloud,

I keep getting brief images of myself,
Is this a dream, is it a vision,
I'm not sure what you're telling me to do,
Is this going to come to fruition?

Who are those people in my dream?
I haven't seen any of them before,
Are they waiting on me to fulfill something?
God, what do you have in store?

Can you keep your voice down to a whisper?
I have to get up in an hour,
Try explaining to my manager,
That I can't sleep because of a higher power,

God, what am I to do,
Please make my vision clear,
I'll try to do what I can to fulfill it,
Cause you won't stay out of my ear,

I know that running is not an option,
When you call, I cannot back down,
Or you'll send me back to the wilderness,
Until my peace is found,

God, please show me the path,
Clear the way and make it plain,
Guide me through my calling,
This I ask in Jesus' name.

Drew added his poem to his folder, lying beside the bed. Minutes later, he drifted into a deep sleep. When he awakened at 4:30, he felt as if he had slept for hours.

Every day Drew wrote poems. Sometimes he would write five poems a day, and store them in his folder. He had separated his "Every Day without You" poems with a folder of poems that he named "The Calling". Both folders were filled with almost four hundred pages of poems. He had dated all of the pages, and stored them by date. Therefore, the order in which they were written could not be mistaken.

It was September 10th, and Tamara had been sleeping in the guestroom for over seven months. A little more than a month ago, Alana had started first grade. Every day Tamara had awakened to fix Alana's hair, and prepare her meal before seeing her off to school.
On this day, Drew had awakened late. He grabbed his folders, and stored them under his cover on the bed. He had just enough time to brush his teeth, take a light shower, put on his clothes, and kiss Alana. Having twenty minutes to get to work, he left, forgetting his lunch, not making his bed, and leaving all of the lights on in his room.
Tamara awakened shortly, thinking that Drew was still there.
"Drew?" She called from the entrance of his room.
"Drew, are you okay?"
There was no response. She walked around in his room, turning off his lights. Noticing that Drew hadn't made his bed she began to pull the covers back. The folders were still underneath Drew's cover. Tamara grabbed both of the folders, and sat them on Drew's dresser. As she sat them down, she noticed that he had named both of them. "Every Day without You" was the folder that caught her eye. She grabbed a couple of pages, and began to read. Reading the first two poems brought back memories for Tamara. She began to cry, understanding that feeling that a person gets when someone walks out of their life without reason. The more she read, the more she cried. She returned the pages to the folder, storing them the same way she retrieved them. She couldn't believe Drew had written so many poems. She knew that his heart was broken when Salida left, but Drew didn't express himself often. Usually his feelings were hidden. After reading the first few, she desired to read them all. She checked the last few pages in the folder, noticing that he had just written two poems the previous night. So bad she wanted to keep reading, but she knew that she had to start on Alana's hair. She made Drew's bed, and laid the folders on top.

Tamara rushed to get everything together. She knew exactly how long it would take her to finish Alana's hair, clean her up, and prepare breakfast for both of them. Her desire to continue reading the poems was so strong that she washed Alana, and put her hair in a ponytail. She placed sausage on the griddle, added two slices of bread to the toaster, and cooked a few eggs. Putting the sausage on the griddle allowed her to prepare breakfast in half the amount of time.

As Alana ate, Tamara readied herself for work. When they were finished, she wiped the dishes off, and put them in the dish washer. Tamara had thirty minutes left. She turned on the television for Alana to watch a show, while she headed to Drew's room to read.

Tamara was so appalled by Drew's poems that she couldn't stop reading them. As she read, she skimmed through the folder to see how things had changed from the first day to how things were currently. She noticed that all of the poems were progressive as if Drew was slowly getting over Salida. She checked the time. She had ten minutes left to get Alana out the door. She closed the folder, and checked to make sure everything had been turn off. While waiting on the bus, she thought of how Drew's poems could help others that were dealing with the same issue. She wasn't sure if Drew was okay with putting himself on display, but she was certain that anyone that read those poems could find healing in some way.

That night, when she came in from work, she noticed that Drew wasn't as upbeat as usual. However, Alana was. Tamara smiled as soon as Alana ran out of the room. Alana held up a sheet of paper. "I colored this for you!"

"Awe, it's so cute! Thank you!"

"You're welcome!" Alana was so proud of her work of art. "I have to finish my homework now. I'll be back later."

"Okay."

Alana returned to her room. Drew headed towards his also.

She asked, "How was work?"

"The same as it always is." He continued walking.

"Drew, what's wrong?"

"Can you come here for a minute?"

"Sure."

The two of them walked into his room. Drew closed the door. Both of the folders were still sitting on the bed. "Did you go through my folders?"

Tamara wanted to lie, but she had never been able to lie to Drew. "I did read some of them."

"This is none of your business! You shouldn't have even been in my room!"

Tamara was shocked. Drew had never yelled at her before. "I only came in because your lights were on. I thought you were still here. I decided to make your bed for you, but the folders were under your sheets."

"Yes, and you should have left them there, and walked away! You had no business in my room, reading anything!"

Fearfully, Tamara said, "Drew, please calm down. I have never heard you talk like this." She continued, "I know that I shouldn't have read your poems, but once I started, I couldn't stop. They were that amazing. I never knew that you could write poems." Drew sat on the bed with his head in his hands as Tamara continued. "Honestly, I didn't get to read them all, but I would love to. To know that someone else understands that feeling that you get when someone walks out of your life without cause, without considering your feelings, or that they are okay with hurting you, it was a healing experience for me." Tears ran down Tamara's face as she continued talking, "I was able to read your poems for about thirty minutes, and felt as if you were walking in my shoes. Please don't be mad at me for that. I have never been able to get over what my ex did to me, how he made me feel, and how he would laugh at the fact that he could manipulate me at any time. Your writings show progress. My life shows someone that has been scarred, someone that hasn't cared to love again. You see that I never gave the guy that I met a chance. I've been hurting for a long time. Drew, I want to love again." Tamara began to walk out of the room, but Drew grabbed her arm. "I'm sorry for yelling at you. I was upset. You know that I hardly ever express the way that I feel about things like this to anyone."

"I know. However, your poems can heal so many people. I read a few of the poems in "The Calling" folder. What you are feeling is not something that happens on a daily basis for most people. For those that have experienced it, your writings will surely help them. Please, talk to someone about getting those poems published."

Drew frowned, "Published! Are you kidding me?"

"I'm not. Have you not considered that this is your calling? How many people do you know that sit around, writing poems only to hide them? Share this with as many people as you possibly can."

Drew considered what Tamara was saying. "Tam, I wouldn't even know where to start."

"I'll go online, and see what we can do. I won't do it unless you okay it."

"First, tell me what you find out."

She agreed, "I'll let you know as soon as I finish my research."

Changing the subject, Drew asked, "Are you ready to eat?"

"I'm starving, but I'm so excited about this that I don't even feel like eating!"

Drew laughed. "Okay, let's eat."

Immediately after eating dinner, Tamara headed to her room to conduct her research. Drew gave Alana a bath, and headed to Tamara's room to see if she had found anything.

"I think that you need to get a copyright, first."

"Okay."

"Once you do that, you can decide as to whether or not you want to do this on your own, or have someone else to do it. The difference is the cost. Plus, the publishers already know what to do."

Drew weighed his options, but realized that he was clueless. "How do I get the copyright?"

Drew felt more and more confident every day. He had never considered writing anything to have it published. However, his job situation seemed to have worsened. Daniel Fakkas was under pressure, and had increased everyone's workload. He was also trying to find a way to pass the pressure onto Bradley. Everyone seemed to have noticed the difference in Daniel's attitude. This caused the workplace to become very stressful.

It was December 4th. Drew made it to work just in time. He turned on his computer, and logged in. Because of the slowness he was experiencing when opening the program he normally uses, he decided to check his email. The new director had emailed everyone the previous day, stating that Daniel Fakkas was no longer employed with the company. Drew grimaced slightly. He didn't feel the need to celebrate. Instead, he felt like praying. As others began to come in, he could hear many rejoicing over the fact. Drew continued working, wondering if things would be better or worse. Considering the fact that Bradley was still there, didn't bring Drew much pleasure. He knew that Daniel's departure would only lead the way for Bradley to become even more arrogant. Even with knowing this, Drew still felt at peace. Something told him that, in due time, everything was going to change for him.

Two days after receiving the copyright, Tamara began to send Drew's poems to multiple publishers to see which would make the best offer. She never expected to receive so many responses. Some responses came within minutes of her emailing a vast majority of the poems. One of the publishers, Gregory Atwater, contacted Drew immediately, but Tamara answered.

"Hello?"

"Yes, could you connect me to Mr. Andrew Davison?"

"He's not in at the moment. Can I assist you?"

"My name is Gregory Atwater, and I just received an email with numerous poems. I would like to set a date to meet with him about getting these poems published."

"I sent those poems out for him. He stepped out for a moment, but he'll be home in ten minutes or so."

"Is there any way that we can meet tonight? I'm sure that if you sent it to me, you probably sent them to other publishers also."

"I did. When he returns, I'll see if he wants to meet tonight. Is the number that is showing on my phone, the number that I should call?"

"Yes ma'am."

"Okay. I'll call, and let you know what he decides."

"Thank you!"

Tamara hung up. Gregory seemed really down to earth. Many of the other publishers had automatic emails set up to respond.

Drew walked through the door not long after Tamara had hung up the phone. He noticed that she was grinning from ear to ear. "What have you done now?"

"There is a publisher that wants to meet with you tonight. Would you like to go?"

"Seriously? Of course I want to go!"

"Tamara called Gregory, and made arrangements to meet him at the nearest restaurant in thirty minutes as his office was only twelve minutes away from Drew's house."

Tamara and Alana sat in a booth, eating ice cream as Drew talked to Gregory. Tamara could only hear small portions of Drew's conversation. However, she realized that Gregory's interest was extreme. He had informed Drew that he was dealing with this same situation, and that every poem that Drew had written expresses the way that he was currently feeling. He made an offer, but Drew advised that he would like to sleep on it. He knew that Drew was waiting to hear from other publishers, and advised that whatever they offered, he would try his best to do better. Gregory, then, shook hands with Drew, and left.

Drew walked over to the table to sit with Tamara and Alana.

"So, how did it go?"

"I really hated to tell him that I needed to sleep on it. He was really emotional about the writings, so much that the hair on my arms was starting to rise."

"Wow!"

"You know how you're in the presence of someone that is truly anointed, and you can feel their spirit? That's how I felt when he was talking to me. He wasn't afraid to talk about his relationship with God."

Tamara was in awe with what Drew had to say about Gregory. Gregory was very attractive, and Tamara knew that it was very hard to come across someone that was as attractive and humble as Drew. Drew's conversation about Gregory almost sounded as if he was talking about himself.

Tamara checked her emails after they had returned. She had received numerous offers from multiple publishers. Several had even asked to meet Drew. She decided that she would call during her lunch the following day.

By the end of the week, Drew had spoken with more than fifty publishers, but none of them gave him the same feeling that Gregory Atwater had given him. Some also made better offers, but, at the time, Drew was certain that he was going to stick with Gregory.

A week before Christmas, Drew had a signing for his new book Every Day without You. Within two hours, Drew had sold more than five hundred books, and more people were standing outside, waiting to get in. Most of them were women that just wanted to meet him for themselves. However, a lot of men also showed up for the signing. Some of the men already knew Drew. Others were men that purchased the book to show support. Drew never expected such a large turnout.

He, Tamara, and Alana headed home for Christmas. Days before his first signing, he had sent two books home, one for his mother and father, the other was for their pastor. After reading his first book, his mother called to let him know that his pastor wanted to offer his book to members in the church. Therefore, after opening gifts Christmas day, Drew headed to the church for another signing.

Over the next two weeks, Drew's books sold like wildfire. Then, on January 5th, he had another signing for his book THE CALLING. Because so many people enjoyed the poems from the first book, even more showed up for THE CALLING. During the signing for THE CALLING, Drew ran out of books. He promised that he would have another signing, but assured everyone that they could also go online to order a copy of the book. He assured them that he would sign those books also.

On December 30th, he had sent two books home, wanting his parents and pastor to have them before anyone. It took Drew's parents no time to read THE CALLING. Drew's writing seemed to add fuel to the fire that the pastor already had in him. He purchased numerous copies to send to other pastors.

Drew's income increased drastically. Sales from THE CALLING had bypassed the sales from his first book. His emails and Facebook friends also increased. So many people sent emails, stating how they found healing from his first book. The issues were not only from having someone to end the relationship. They were also from dealing with the loss of a loved one. Some even found comfort from not being able to see close friends that were incarcerated.

His second book was deeper. Therefore, his emails came in with power. There were times in which he could almost feel the spirit of the sender. At times, he had to step away from his computer because of the strength of the message. His writings caused many people to pray for him, and he tried to read every email. He printed and stored his most powerful messages in a special folder that he named "Motivation".

Over the next few months, Drew's life had changed. Friends began to make frequently visits to his house for any reason they could think of. However, Drew continued with his normal routine as if this never happened. He continued working, cooking on a daily basis, and writing poems. He sat aside thirty-five minutes a day to read his messages. This only motivated him to write more.

Tamara also noticed that Drew's routine hadn't changed. However, he seemed to mature with every poem that he had written, and he allowed her to read every one of them.

Because of the relationship he had obtained with Drew, Tamara was now dating Gregory Atwater. Not for a second was Gregory cautious of Drew's relationship with Tamara. He completely understood the circumstances, and had also become drawn to Alana. At times, he and Tamara would take Alana out with them, so that Drew could have time alone.

After finishing his third book, Drew realized that there was more for him to do. He began to develop a business plan as he was tired of answering to people that never really cared for his presence. He decided against purchasing a new car. He knew that with time, that would come. He became more and more focused on finding a way to become his own boss.

On June 5th, Drew presented a business model to the financial department at his bank. There was a building for rent, located in the heart of the downtown area. He decided that he wanted to open a restaurant in the area. They looked over all of the details, realizing that Drew had truly done his research. Drew advised that it would take him two months to get everything together. He considered this time because he was still working, and needed to find workers that would assist with the opening. A week later, after much research, the financial department approved the loan, using Drew's account balance as equity. His account balance had bypassed the amount that he needed for the loan. Therefore, the approval wasn't a problem.

On July 12th, Drew put in a four week notice. He didn't tell them where he was going or what he was doing. He only let them know that he was leaving the company. Bradley Southerland walked over to Drew's desk. "Are you leaving because you wrote those books?"
"No, I just have other things that I desire to do."
"Like what?"
"I don't really want to talk about it."
"Those writings aren't going to pay for things forever. You might want to reconsider putting in your notice if that's the case."
Drew said nothing as he continued to work. Bradley stood over Drew for a little longer, waiting for a response from Drew. Still, Drew said nothing. Bradley's advice only encouraged Drew to work harder.
Every day after work, Drew would pick up Alana and head over to the building. Tamara would stop by the building to pick up Alana after she left work. Drew worked hard to have the building prepared for the grand opening. Now and then, without charge, Drew's friends would stop by to assist him with his preparations. Drew thanked God for his friends.

Each day became a challenge as Bradley pestered Drew over and over. Two weeks before Drew's last day, Bradley sent out a notice to everyone in regards to Drew's departure. Many walked over to his desk to congratulate him. Others that were closer to Drew insisted on having him keep in touch with them. Drew wanted to include many of the workers in his exit plan, but was uncertain as to how he could help them. Instead, he invited them all to come and eat at "Bill and Emma's", a restaurant that he had named after his grandparents. They all reassured him that they would be there.

Closure

152

It was Drew's last day of working for the company in which he had been working for more than eight years. Fabio Bradley Southerland emailed Drew, asking him to come to his office. On his way to Bradley's office, Drew grabbed papers that he had printed days earlier. When Drew walked into the office, along with Bradley sat the new director that had terminated Daniel.

"Yes sir?"

"Come and have a seat, Drew."

Drew sat facing the two of them.

Bradley began, "Is there anything you would like to say as you are stepping out of your position."

Drew hesitated, but realized that if he said nothing, his point would have never been proven.

"Yes, there is."

He handed the printed copies to Bradley.

"What is this?"

"These are emails from other coworkers, practices, and Daniel."

"Why are you giving them to me?"

"Because I want you to realize that the whole time you were throwing salt at me, I was doing everything to help you, and everyone under you. Most of these are emails from my coworkers that needed assistance with balancing. There's one from Daniel that asks me to stop helping so that he could let his boss know that you weren't doing your job to properly train the other employees. There's also the email in which you attacked me in regards to posting $30,000 to the General Ledger, without ever asking me why this was done; only to find that my posting was correct. There's other emails that I had sent to you to inform you that one of our clients was stealing money. You didn't respond until it was too late.

You've been throwing salt on me for years, but I've been helping you this whole time. I've even had to go behind your trainers to assist in training new employees. I didn't get paid for that.

There are other emails from coworkers, asking me to apply for a higher position. I checked the website, only to find that I wasn't even considered for the positions in which I applied. I was informed that you were the reason why.

I brought these papers here to thank you. Thank you, because you made it impossible for me to move up, but it also made me work harder to fulfill God's purpose. The amount of money I have made in the past seven years isn't even close to the amount of money I've made from my writings. God was calling me and calling me, but I had become content with my status here. I didn't think I could ever move up because everyone was contacting you whenever I applied for something different."

Drew shook his head, "But God.... my God allowed me to move up, and move out of the situation I was in. Walking into what He had in store for me caused me to not have to answer to anyone but Him." He turned to Bradley, "Can you imagine how that feels: not having to answer to anyone but God?"

Drew stood with his head up, "Thank you so much for rejection."

Bradley said nothing. He didn't make an attempt to look at the new director. Instead, he sat, reading the papers that were given to him by Drew. Bradley felt like an ass.

The new director, Austin Phillips, walked out of Bradley's office without a word.

Drew returned to his seat, and completed his last day. He knew he had a long road ahead of him, but the feeling he received with knowing that he was only days away from opening his own business brought him an overwhelming amount of joy.

After celebrating his last day of work, Drew busied himself with the restaurant. He finished painting, installed two registers, and added chairs and tables. The menu covers that he had ordered also came in. Drew slid the menus into the covers, and took a look at the building. "God this is it. This is the building that I would see from time to time before I slept."

Over the next ten days, Drew spent his time going over everything that was needed in order to run his business successfully. He even had Alana, Tamara, and Gregory to pretend that they were customers, wanting to place an order. He would make dinner at the restaurant, and bring it out to them. Gregory was always amazed with every meal. He was sure that he would tell all of his friends about the restaurant.

Drew was certain that everything was ready. He gave the three a tour throughout the building. They couldn't believe the size of Drew's office. Gregory stated, "This looks more like a small home."

Drew replied, "I'll be here most of the time, preparing meals, and finding new flavors to add to the menu. I had to make it look like home."

The four of them headed out of the building that Thursday. Drew decided that he would rest on Friday, as the doors would open on Saturday.

It was seven o'clock in the morning, Saturday, August 24th. Drew's family stood at the front door of the building in which Drew had rented. Everyone was ready to walk in, and start cooking.

Drew opened the door with tears in his eyes. He hugged everyone as they walked in. Everyone seemed to be just as anxious and nervous as Drew. He couldn't wait to see how many people would show up for his first day as the doors were to open at eleven for lunch.

At ten, Drew's brother's friends from his motorcycle club were knocking at the door of the building. Drew walked to the door. He noticed some of the faces in the crowd.

"Hey Walter, what's going on?"

"Well, your brother told us that you might need a little help on your first day. So, we brought the whole crew down to help out."

"Are you kidding me?"

"Seriously, we brought our podium down to set up for valet parking. We brought our suites so that we can look good when opening the doors for the ladies. You know we like the ladies!" Walter raised his hands, "We just want to help out. We're not asking for anything. We didn't have anything to do anyway."

Drew put his hands over his face. He couldn't believe this was happening to him. "I really appreciate this." He shook hands with all of the men as they set up the podium, and headed to Drew's office to change into their attire. Drew walked to his personal bathroom to have a talk with God. "God you know I wasn't expecting this. I have my best friend that brought in people that volunteered to be waiters and waitresses. I have my family that just showed up to assist. Now, I have valet, and hosts!" Drew clenched his fist, "How can I thank you for this?" He threw his hand towards his office. "These people are asking for nothing! They just showed up!" Shaking his head, he asked, "God, How-Can-I-Thank-You-For-This? In Jesus' name I pray, Amen." He wiped the tears from his eyes, and headed back to the kitchen. He called everyone to the front door for prayer. He looked around the room at everyone that came to assist. Everyone looked amazingly professional. Everyone seemed ready. Drew wished that he could run back to the bathroom. He bowed his head, and others followed. "My God," Drew shook his head. Tamara and Celia began to cry as they could feel Drew's spirit in those two words. His father patted his back as tears flowed from Drew's face. Drew continued with his head bowed. "I don't know what more I can say. I feel as if thank you is just not enough. To see that with just stepping out on what you asked of me, to look at this building, to see all of these faces that are before me, here to help me with what you have called me to do, thank you cannot be enough."

No one could hold back a tear when listening to Drew's prayer of God's exceeding grace. As Drew prayed, fists tightened among the crew. When, Drew finished, everyone had made up in their mind that they would do their best to make this the best day that Drew could ever have.

At a quarter until eleven, the parking lot was packed. Drew had opened the doors when he noticed that many were arriving early. He never expected for so many people to show up. Now and then, he would peep out to see if the crowd was dying down. It never slowed. Even Drew's overflow area was filled. When advised that they would have to wait, no one left.

Tamara was doing a great job as the hostess, switching out with another volunteer only to take or give breaks to others. Her beauty was acknowledged by many of the men and women. Displaying her amazing smile put almost everyone at ease as she greeted those that entered.

Around six that night, Austin Phillips walked up to Tamara.

"Good evening! How may I assist you?" asked Tamara.

"Good evening! I am looking for Andrew."

"He's actually in the kitchen cooking. Is there anything in which I can assist you?"

"I just wanted to see him for just a second."

"Okay. If you can give me just a second, I'll see if he is available. What is your name?"

"My name is Austin Phillips."

"Okay, I'll be right back."

Tamara called the backup hostess to assist as she stepped away to find Drew. Drew was assisting his mother when Tamara walked in.

"Hey, there's someone named Aundrey Phelps that wants to speak with you."

"Do you mean Austin Phillips?"

"Yeah... whatever.... He wants to speak to you."

"Okay."

Drew washed his hands, removed his apron, and headed out to meet Austin. Austin smiled as Drew stepped out of the kitchen. Drew walked over to Austin, and held out his hand. Austin returned the favor.

"How are you doing sir," asked Drew.

"I'm great! I wanted to congratulate you personally. The food was nothing short of amazing! I'll probably gain around five pounds as I have eaten so much tonight."

"Well, I am glad you enjoyed it."

"Yes, I did! I also wanted to tell you that I have an amazing amount of respect for you as you have put up with so much. I walked back into Bradley's office, and grabbed some of the papers that you had printed." Austin shook his head. "I could not believe the things I had read. He never backed you up on anything, never read your emails on time, and gave you a hard time when you tried to take off for your sick child. What Bradley had done to you was very unacceptable."

Andrew smiled, "That's all behind me now. We don't even have to talk about it. I just hope that you enjoyed your food, and will consider returning at some time in the near future."

"You bet I will! As a matter of fact, I was wondering if you could cater some of the events at work. Your old coworkers would probably love to know that the opportunity to enjoy your food still exists."

Drew agreed, "I can do that. You'll have to let me know when. I haven't printed any business cards, but they are on the way."

"No need to rush! I will definitely be back."

Drew laughed, "Okay... well, I have to get back in the kitchen to help my mother." Drew shook hands with Austin again. "Thanks for coming out!" "No problem!"

It was eleven thirty, and the restaurant was set to close at midnight. Some people were still waiting to be seated as they had arrived late. Drew advised the bikers not to allow anyone else through the doors as he wanted to allow everyone enough time to rest. He and the entire crew were exhausted, but the time had gone by so fast due to the large crowd. Even with being tired, everyone was excited. The tips for their service reassured them that they should return.

That night, after Drew had made it home, he closed the door of his room, and began to write:

Nothing Short

Sometimes we ask God "why",

Thinking He made a mistake,

We want him to correct the wrong,

Not understanding that it was fate,

God is a merciful father,

In our hearts we have a song,
For His grace and His forgiveness,
But mostly, for His existence alone,

He's nothing short of omniscient,
He knows all of our thoughts and iniquities,
He turns around our bad situations,
As soon as we fall to our knees,

He nothing short of omnipotent,
He holds the world in His hand,
He created such beautiful scenery,
For all of the wretched people living in this land,

He's nothing short of omnipresent,
He's there for all of us, He sees our fall,
So why do we run from Him,
When we can clearly hear His call,

God, I just want to say "Thank you",
For the inner peace, oh how you make me feel free,
You open doors when I don't deserve it,
You're nothing short of wonderful to me.

Afterwards, Drew slept.

Every day more and more people poured into the restaurant. Some became regulars. In no time, Drew had become familiar with the regulars. He loved seeing them just as much as they loved eating his food. When trying new flavors, he made sure that they were some of the first to try. He enjoyed their feedback, and the relationship he had created.

A few months after Alana turned 8, Drew decided that he would like to ask Jewel Lowe out on a date. She came into the restaurant with a few of her friends from time to time. He hadn't dated in such a long time. He contemplated his approach, but figured that simply asking her would be enough. Although he knew he was ready, something in his heart was telling him that he still needed closure. He knew where Salida was, and how to contact her. He just didn't know how she would respond to him. He began to dial her number, but stopped. Instead, he sent her a text: Can we talk? Sure: was her response. I want to talk face to face: was his reply. She replied: no problem. Where, when? He replied: 2 wks, want to take a trip, get us away from the town, maybe for 2 days. K. Will be ready: was her response.

He decided that after this was over, he would move on, start a new chapter in his life with someone else, and continue working on ways to improve his business.

After opening the restaurant, Drew had gained twenty pounds. He knew that he needed to get rid of the weight. He made up in his mind that he would start working out again to at least take off ten of those pounds before he met with Salida. He was never an overweight guy, and those twenty pounds didn't cause him to seem unattractive. The women were still swarming. Immediately, he decided that he would begin to work out for, at least, two hours before he left for work. Not having to open the restaurant until 11 would allow him the time he needed to go to the gym after Alana caught the bus.

Two weeks and ten pounds later, Drew stopped by Salida's to pick her up. He texted her to let her know that he was outside. Seconds later, Salida was walking towards the car. She seemed even more beautiful than the last time he had seen her. She wore a fitted shirt, and a pair of skinny jeans that fit perfectly, revealing much of what Drew loved about her.

"Why'd she have to wear that? She's cheating," he mumbled to himself.

As she entered the car, she managed a smile, "Hey!"

"Hey! How have you been?"

"I'm fine. You?"

"All is well."

"How's Alana?"

How can you ask about your own child, and not even want to see her? He thought to himself. "She's great, just growing up."

"I'm sure."

Drew turned up the music. Feeling anger building in himself, he decided that he wasn't so sure that this was a great idea after all. However, he continued driving. He knew that he had to get this off of his chest in order for him to move forward. For the first thirty minutes of the drive, he kept telling himself that this was needed.

Salida sat silently during the ride, glaring out the window the same as she used to when Drew would drive a long distance. He knew that she would think herself to sleep. Slowly, she drifted after adjusting her seat. He watched her the same way he used to watch her before.

He did notice a difference this time. She seemed uneasy as she looked out the window earlier. As if she was afraid someone was watching her leave. He shook the thought off, thinking that if Jonathan was there, he never would have let her leave.

Drew tried to get the thought of Jonathan out of his mind. That one man had ruined his life for some years now. Drew didn't know what he would have done if he would have seen Jonathan come out of the house behind Salida.

As he thought, he glanced at her, asking himself, *how does this one man have such a stronghold over her? I understand that they had a son, but we have a daughter to nurture. Her son isn't even here.* Feeling guilty about his thought, he began to focus on the road again.

Salida didn't awaken until they had reached their destination. Drew checked in, carrying all of the bags himself. She stood in the lobby quietly, discreetly observing her surroundings. She loved the lobby of this particular hotel, and thought the food was pretty amazing also.

He decided that they would spend the first day out and about before they discussed everything. He also wanted to get a drink under their belts to put both of them at ease for the discussion.

As the two of them entered the room, Salida turned to Drew.

"Will you make love to me now?"

He looked at her, almost disgusted with her comment. But, after seeing the fire in her eyes, he knew she was sincere. She headed in his direction, ready to take her shirt off at any moment. Drew reached for her, tempted to reply, feeling the arousal in himself. Instead of starting something that they would both enjoy, he stopped her.

"This is not why we are here."

"You don't want to make love to me?"

He stared into her eyes, shaking his head.

"We're here because we have things to discuss. I want to enjoy my time while we're here, but we really do need to talk."

"Okay."

Salida sat on the bed with her head down, trying to calm herself. She had always been turned on by getting away, and staying in nice hotels with him. Plus, Drew smelled so good, and he wore a shirt that revealed just enough of his chest to ensure her that he had been working out. She watched as he hung his clothes, and put the bags in the closet.

"I actually came up to bring the clothes in the room, but I'm really hungry. Let's go grab a bite to eat," stated Drew as he finished putting the bags in the closet.

"Okay. I'm a little hungry myself."

"What would you like to eat?"

"Right now, anything is cool."

"Well, the bags are in the closet. I'm ready when you are."

Both decided on Italian. They sat at the restaurant, eating, drinking wine, and chatting away about what was going on in their life. Drew tried to mention Alana as less as possible, thinking that a discussion about her would only upset him. He managed to work his way around discussing her, although she was all that he knew.

Afterwards, he decided that they could take a walk downtown and enjoy the life of the city.

They spent the rest of the day laughing, talking, and listening to live music in a few bars that Drew had heard about. Later, they headed back to the room. Salida was slightly intoxicated from a few of the drinks she had consumed, but felt comfortable because she knew that Drew would take care of her. As they entered the room, she fell across the bed. Well enough for Drew to understand, she blurted out, "Thank you for such a wonderful night. I am so exhausted, and haven't been out like that in a long time. I really appreciate that you asked me to come."

"Not a problem. I just wanted us to get away."

She sat on the bed, watching as he began to remove his shirt. Saliva seemed to flow from all directions as she watched. The liquor didn't help. She was so ready to attack him, wanting to do whatever she could to arouse him, longing for him to be inside her.

Drew could feel her stare. He knew that he was turning her on. He could feel it. "I'm about to shower."

Damn, she thought, but said, "Okay, I'll go after you."

Drew jumped in the shower, trying to clear his head. He knew what she would have done if he had removed everything. He wasn't here for that, but he was turned on by her. Taking the shower gave him time to calm down, time away from her, time to think of what he would say to assure her that closure was needed. He decided to take as much time as needed in the shower.

Salida, angered by how much time he was taking to get out of shower, laid her head on the pillow, and dozed. She knew he would awaken her when he was out.

He didn't. Instead, he grabbed some loungewear and went downstairs to the lobby to sit for a while, needing some time alone as she slept. He realized that sleeping was hard when trying to find closure with someone that made you feel as if you couldn't love anyone else as much. Drew grabbed a magazine, and began to read a few articles about successful business owners, how they differentiated themselves, and what made them continue to search for other ways to implement their growing company.

Salida awakened to realize that she was alone. Instead of going to look for Drew, she showered, hoping he would come back as soon as she stepped out of the shower, and began to apply lotion. He did. He entered the room at that very moment. Instead of tackling her as he would have done before, he walked over to the window, looking out, and waiting for her to put on her clothes.

"Are you okay?"

"Yes. I just had a few things on my mind; went downstairs for a minute."

"Oh."

"Salida, I brought you here because I wanted to get some things out of my head. I'm not sure what I did for you to leave us. I just wanted clarity on it. I want to know what caused you to totally walk away from us."

"It was nothing you did. It was me. Can you come and sit?"

Drew walked away from the window, and headed towards Salida. He didn't realize how much he was still hurting until now. He refused his tears, but his face was readable.

"Drew, I'm really sorry for walking out on you and Alana. I honestly didn't think I was worthy of having the two of you in my life. Jonathan made me feel that way. He came to my job about a month before her fifth birthday. Told me how sorry I was for trying to move on after killing our first child." Tears began to flow down Salida's face as she continued, "He made me feel that I wasn't worthy. You two were the best thing that had ever happened to me after losing my son. So, I walked away because I didn't want to mess things up. I couldn't stomach the thought of losing you or Alana."

Salida, now sobbing, said, "The three of us were so happy. When Jonathan showed up, I realized that I still loved him. So, I left. Walking away from you and Alana was hard. But, I was afraid that Jonathan would do something to ruin things for us since he blamed me for Chris' death."

Drew grabbed Salida, "Did he threaten to do something?"

"No. It was the anger he showed when he stared at a picture of the three of us."

"Why didn't you tell me?"

"Because, I didn't want you to think I was seeing him. You would have had hundreds of questions about him that I couldn't answer."

Drew knew that Salida wasn't being honest about everything. "Do you still love him?"

"Not like that. I love you. I didn't want to get you involved. Since the day I met you, we've had no major issues. I just wanted to leave it that way."

Agitatedly Drew said, "Do you think walking out on us helped to clear anything? I had thousands of questions in my head. I called you, you wouldn't answer. You were never home. You never told me, your own husband, that you had changed jobs. I couldn't find you to even get an explanation on what was going on. And Alana..." Drew's anger began to rise. Tears began to flow from nowhere. "Alana was asking me where you were, and when you were coming home every day. Do you know how it feels to tell your daughter that you don't know when her mommy is coming back? She began to sleep in the bed with me, waiting to see you. For months this went on. You've missed so much, her first day of school, birthdays, losing her teeth, riding her bike for the first time. You've missed it all for something that could have been handled if you would have just told me what was going on."

Salida sat on the bed, crying, thinking about everything she'd missed in Alana's life. "Drew, I'm so sorry."

Drew, sitting across from Salida, rolled on top of her, kissing her so intensely. She kissed back, longing for this moment. She knew it wouldn't be passionate, he was too angry. He kissed her hard, and sucked her bottom lip. She moaned, ensuring him that this was needed. He could feel her heat increasing between her legs as he lied between them. One stroke of his manhood against her put her in a trance.

"Please take me."

He concurred, rising to pull off her underwear, and pull his own pants down. Seeing what she knew was there, longing for it, she moaned again. Her longing showed all over her face. Tears, once formed from hurt, now of zeal flowed from her eyes. He entered her. She gasped. "Oh Drew!" He shook his head, trying to clear his mind of the excitement he felt inside of her walls. Drew continued throughout the night, taking what he wanted until there was nothing left in him to give, putting Salida to sleep like a hibernating bear.

The next morning, Salida's snoring awakened both of them.

"Sorry, but you drained me of all of my energy last night."

He kissed her forehead, "It's okay."

Feeling the cold air on her naked body, Salida began to shiver. Drew pulled her close, allowing her to warm herself from his body. She laid her head on his chest, slowly drifting back to sleep. Drew lied there as she slept, thinking about when this was the norm for them.

The remaining portion of the trip was just as great as the beginning. Salida never mentioned the opening of the restaurant to Drew. She wanted him to tell her about it, but he never mentioned it. She knew that he wasn't one to boast, but she believed that he would at least mention it. Because he never mentioned it, she didn't think it was doing well.

She watched him often as they headed back, not believing that he would attempt to let her back in his life. She knew he had a sore spot for her, but could never come to grips with why he cared so much about her. She had lied to him, cheated on him, and left him in a financial bind. She knew it was wrong. Even the lovemaking was wrong. She enjoyed sleeping with him as he was very passionate. But, she loved it even more when he was angry or hurting.

Drew thought that the trip had changed things. He was under the assumption that Salida would return, especially after their talk, but she didn't. Instead, she stopped answering his text and never checked to see if things were okay.

A week after Drew's trip, Gregory approached Drew to advise that he was ready to propose to Tamara. Drew was so happy for her. He couldn't believe that Tamara had finally let go of her feelings for Shaun, and had moved on with Gregory.

Tamara and Gregory married the following year. She was never close to a lot of women. Therefore, Alana was her maid-of-honor. Drew and Tamara also sang a song that was written by Drew. His fingers against the piano left everyone in a trance. The crowd was in tears by the end of the song.

Two months after the honey-moon, Tamara found out that she was pregnant. She became very emotional as she never expected to have any children. She called Alana to let her know, and asked if she would like to help out. Alana loved the idea, and agreed to help. She knew that Tamara was not her mother, but she also knew that they would always be a part of each other's life.

Eventually, Drew began to date Jewel Lowe. He took things very slow with her as he wanted to be sure that they were compatible. However, he enjoyed getting to know more about her, loving that she was always willing to try something new with him. Even when things didn't go as planned, they were still able to laugh, realizing that the trip wouldn't have been as fun without the mishap. There were many mishaps, from falling into water, wasting food all over the place, and getting stuck in the mud. There were pictures taken for every mishap, causing them to enjoy every moment together.

Salida realized that Drew had been getting along well without her. His name grew more and more after the opening of his restaurant. She had been tempted to pay him a visit, but she wasn't sure how he would react when he saw her. Many of her girlfriends frequented the restaurant, always talking about how attractive the owner was. They had invited her a few times, but she declined.
Eventually, after the constant invitations from her friends, she decided the she would go. She called her friend Cilia.
"Hey Cil."
"Hey, what's up?"
"We should have a girl's night at that place called Bill and Emma's that you all have been telling me about."
"Okay, that's cool. Plus, the girls will love it. They love going to that place."
"Okay, let's go on Friday."
"Alright, I've wanted you to see that guy anyway. I know you already have your share of men on hand, but he's pretty amazing."
"Okay, well let me check out the dresses in my closet."
After hanging up with Cilia, Salida checked her closet for something really nice. The girls had seen her in almost everything in her closet. She wanted to look her best. One reason was to impress Drew. Another was so that she could make sure he recognized her out of the group. She decided to go shopping.
Friday night, the girls loaded up in Salida's SUV. As she pulled into the parking lot, one of the valets assisted all of the women out of the vehicle. He then grabbed her keys to park it. Another guy happily opened the door to the restaurant for them. There was a hostess at the front, directing everyone

to a table. The group had made reservations, so they were all assisted to a larger table that had been prepared for them. Drew walked over to the table.

"Can I get you ladies anything to drink?"

Salida was sitting at the end of the table, and immediately looked up when she heard Drew's voice. Drew noticed Salida, but never focused his attention on her. All of the ladies ordered drinks. Drew was familiar with some of the ladies. He acknowledged the fact that they were regulars, and inquired as to whether or not they were getting the same dish. Most agreed. Some sat, admiring Drew's physique. As Drew walked away to get the drinks, the waitress came over to introduce herself and obtain the orders. Momentarily, Drew returned with the drinks, and was about to head to the office when Salida stopped him.

"Drew, you got a minute?"

"Sure."

The other ladies gasped, not knowing that Salida knew Drew. The two of them headed to his office, Salida with an encouraging walk.

"That heifer knew him all along," exclaimed one of the ladies.

Another lady agreed, "She sure did."

"That's probably why she hasn't been out here," said another.

Cilia sat in dismay, "I didn't know that she knew him either."

They all sat, trying to figure out how Salida and Drew were connected.

In the meantime, Drew and Salida were in his office. Salida looked around.

"This is a nice place. Your office is really large."

"I spend a lot of time here. I knew I would. So, I had them to make it this way."

"Oh. So, how come we never got a chance to go on that boat ride we had talked about the last time you called?"

"I was actually waiting on you to call me back with a date."

"We can go sometime next week."

"I can't."

"Well, let me know when you can."

Drew shook his head, "I can't go at all."

Salida, confused by his response, said "Why?"

"I just can't do that with you anymore."

"What do you mean, Drew?"

"Salida, you've played with my heart for a while now. I really tried. I have given you every opportunity to be there, but you've never taken them. It was all by choice. I've sent text after text. I've called. You either never responded, or you responded days later. I've been waiting on you for a very, long time. You didn't want to be there."

"I did, I just had some things to take care of."

"Salida, that's not an excuse. I have done everything I could possibly do. You asked for some time alone. I gave you time. You told me that you needed to clear some things. I allowed that space. I've been taking care of our child. You haven't even come to see her. You know where we live."

Salida was silent. Drew continued.

"I can't allow you to hurt me anymore. Even when Alana was in my hometown with my parents, you knew. You had every opportunity to come over. Still, I slept alone. My doors were open to you. There has been absolutely nothing to stop you, but you. By choice, you never called, you never showed up. You've been doing your thing." He continued, "So hard, I tried to fix this. I tried to fix us. I've written letters, everything. When we were out of town, you told me that you were still in love with me. You apologized for not being there. We walked through the city, holding hands like married couples do. All that I needed you to do was show up, to show me that you wanted to be there. You didn't. I truly tried to fix us. Then, I realized, WE weren't broken. I was. I allowed you to mentally break me."

Drew shook his head, "No more."

Drew's face was filled with certainty, and Salida acknowledged it. Therefore, she turned to walk away. He concluded, "Don't mistake this for anger. I'm not mad at you at all. You can only do to me what I allow you to do. Just make sure you show up for Alana's graduation."

Salida left the office. Drew felt a peace like never before. He closed his eyes, lay back in his chair, and thanked God for the strength to let her go. He grabbed his pen, and began to write:

Stronger

When I first met you,
I knew that something wasn't right,
Your demeanor in the store was extreme,
I still tried to be polite,

My love became stronger for you,
As we spent more and more time together,
The more I learned about you,
The more I thought we would last forever,

I overlooked some things,
I knew that you liked a lot of attention,
I thought that my time with you was enough,
I didn't expect an intervention,

I did my best to keep you by my side,
I even went down on my knees and asked that you be my bride,
To make you the happiest woman, how hard I tried,
I let go of what knew, I swallowed my pride,

Then we had a beautiful daughter,
What a blessing it was to see,
Someone so faultless, so innocent,
Someone produced by you and me,

I was so happy to be a husband, a father, and a son,
I removed the clench with my parents,
So that we could become one,

Then on June 29th,
You walked away from it all,
You left a note on our bed,
You took the photos of us off of the wall,

I tried my best to find you,
I wanted to do everything I could to work this out,
You had planned your exit in advance,
A mother and wife, we were without,

It took a long time for me to get over this,
My whole world had been turned around,
I couldn't find a path worth walking,
Then, God stepped in, and joy I found,

God gave me a peace,
That I couldn't explain,
He was there to cover me,
In the midst of the pain,

Who knew that those poems,
Would be a part of my calling,
So many people have found healing,
When I thought I was falling,

So, I just want to say thank you,
Can't play with my heart any longer,
Walking out on us brought so much pain,
But in the end it made us stronger.

Acknowledgements

First, I would like to thank God for ordering my steps throughout this writing. I knew that I had a desire to write this book, but had no idea exactly what I would put into it. I asked God to lead, but for a long time I had nothing. I asked God, "Why is it that when I log into my computer to write, I have nothing to say?" Mentally, I wasn't fit to finish the writing. Therefore, I abandoned the very thing that I desired.

Now, it's done! Thank you for your patience and your support. I love you all.

I also want to thank my daughter, my mother, my siblings, Carolyn Sanders (my second mom), my family, and all of my friends for the support.

A special thanks to everyone that will purchase this book. I hope that you enjoy reading it as much as I enjoyed writing it. I pray that this book encourages you to make the best choices for yourself. There are always signs to show you whether or not a person is right for you. However, we (including myself) have a tendency to ignore those signs. Stop ignoring them! God has something good for you!

One more thing:

At the time that I was writing this book, I was dealing with some of the issues included in the book myself. I used to hate it when people would state that they couldn't do anything because they were always being held down. I truly believed that many were just using the "Race card".

On January 12th, I awakened around 6 a.m., and felt the need to acknowledge the fact that I love who I am. For those of you that have dealt with racial issues, those of you that always feel like you have to do twice as much to prove that you're capable of doing your job, and those of you that feel as if you just aren't able to make a career advancement because of the color of your skin, check out my poem on the next page.

And always remember: Where there is no vision, the people perish.

Love you!

LaWanda

Embracing Black

What's wrong with me?
Is there a problem with being black?
Is anyone listening to me?
Does anyone have my back?

I embrace being black,
I love the color of my skin,
All of the beauty in one person,
Why do others consider it a sin?

Sin is something wrong,
It's something one has had to hide,
From fornication to homosexuality,
Coveting and pride.

There has never been a day,
Where I could hide the color of my skin,
When I awaken it's always there,
What the hell? Black is in!

I cannot care less what others think,
Ignorance comes with any race,
Arrogance, belligerence, and bigotry,
All can be seen on any face.

For me, I love all,
Skinny, round, or tall,
I love no matter what choices you make.
Whether you're up or down, we all fall.

So, the next time you're in my presence,
And you ever feel the need,
To acknowledge the color of my skin,
Please take heed.

I'm comfortable with being me,

I love the skin God has me in,
If there was ever a time that I could choose,
You better believe; I'd go with this again.

I love it! I love it! I love it!
Every tone, every touch,
From my head to my toes,
I love this skin so much!

Chocolate, caramel, and mocha,
Big-boned, bow-legged, or thin,
There's one thing that'll never be a problem for me,
That's the color of my skin.

Be blessed!

J. Madsei